This book belongs to

Books with pictures by
Gyo Fujikawa

A CHILD'S GARDEN OF VERSES

THE NIGHT BEFORE CHRISTMAS

BABIES

BABY ANIMALS

MOTHER GOOSE

A CHILD'S BOOK OF POEMS

FAIRY TALES AND FABLES

Fairy Tales and Fables

Edited by
Eve Morel

Pictures by Gyo Fujikawa

Grosset & Dunlap • Publishers • New York

Library of Congress Card Number: 70-122562

Copyright © 1970, by Gyo Fujikawa.
All rights reserved under International
and Pan-American Copyright Conventions.
Published simultaneously in Canada.
Printed in the United States of America.
1975 PRINTING
ISBN: 0-448-02814-X (Trade Edition)
ISBN: 0-448-02824-7 (Library Edition)

Contents

Little Red Riding Hood

ONCE upon a time there lived a little girl who had a pretty red cape with a bright red hood. She always wore her red-hooded cape. And that is why she was called Little Red Riding Hood.

One day her mother packed a basket with cakes and fruit. She said to Little Red Riding Hood, "This is a gift for you to take to your grandmother. She is not well and will enjoy some nice cake and fruit."

So Little Red Riding Hood tied on her red cape and hood, and set out for Grandmother's house.

As she was going through the woods, she met a big wolf. The wolf spoke to her in a gruff voice. "Good morning, little girl," he said. "Where are you going with that nice basket of cake and fruit?"

"I am going to visit my grandmother."

"Well, well," said the wolf politely, "I'm going to visit your grandmother, too."

The crafty old wolf knew where Grandmother lived—and so, while Little Red Riding Hood stopped along the way to pick bright flowers, and watch butterflies flitting among the trees, the wicked wolf arrived at Grandmother's house long before she got there. He peeked in the window. He saw Grandmother sitting in her rocking chair, knitting a sweater. But Grandmother saw the wolf, too. She jumped out of the chair, slipped into the clothes closet, and quickly locked the door behind her.

11

The wolf came into the house. He tried to open the closet door, but could not. Then he spied Grandmother's nightcap and shawl hanging on a peg.

"Aha!" he cried. "I'll put on Grandmother's nightcap and shawl, and get into bed. Little Red Riding Hood will think I'm her grandmother."

Pretty soon Little Red Riding Hood knocked on the door.

"Who's there?" said the wolf, pretending to be Grandmother.

"It is I, Grandmother," said Little Red Riding Hood.

"Come in, my dear," said the wolf in his most gentle voice. He drew the covers up around his chin.

"Oh, Grandmother," cried Little Red Riding Hood, standing beside the bed. "What big, bright eyes you have!"

"The better to see you with, my dear," replied the wolf softly.

Little Red Riding Hood came closer. "Oh, Grandmother, what big ears you have!"

"The better to hear you with, my dear," said the wolf, still more softly.

Little Red Riding Hood leaned over the bed. "And, Grandmother, what big teeth you have!" she whispered.

"The better to eat you with!" cried the wolf, and he pushed back the covers and sprang out of bed. Then Little Red Riding Hood saw that it was the wolf pretending to be her grandmother. She screamed with all her might.

At that moment, a woodsman was passing by. He heard Little Red Riding Hood's screams, and broke into the house just in time to save her from the wolf. But the wolf slipped past the woodsman and rushed off into the trees.

"Never mind," said the woodsman. "I'll catch him." And he ran into the woods after the wolf.

Then Grandmother came out of the closet where she had been hiding, and she made a delicious lunch of milk, cake and fruit for Little Red Riding Hood and herself.

They had just sat down to eat when the woodsman came back. "The wolf will never bother you again," he said.

Little Red Riding Hood and her grandmother thanked the woodsman and asked him to stay to lunch. He did so, gladly, for he was very hungry. Afterward, he walked with Little Red Riding Hood through the woods to her mother's house, where she lived happily for many years. But she never met another wolf.

13

14

The Hare and the Tortoise

THE HARE made fun of the tortoise every day. "What a slowpoke you are!" he laughed. "Your legs are so short they never get you anywhere. Just look at my long legs!"

"All the same, if we were to run a race, I would beat you," replied the tortoise.

"That's a good joke!" scoffed the hare. And he ran all around the forest telling everyone how the tortoise was going to beat him in a race.

The fox offered to be the judge, and he marked off the distance and told them when to start.

"On your mark—get set—go!" he cried.

The two started off together, but the hare was soon far out of sight. The tortoise did not mind. He went slowly and steadily on his way.

But the hare very soon grew tired. "I have plenty of time," he told himself. So he stopped to eat clover and drink in the brook. Then he sat down under a shady tree and fell asleep.

Meanwhile, the tortoise plodded slowly along the road. He was hungry, but he did not stop to eat. He was thirsty, but he did not stop to drink. He saw his friends along the way, but he did not stop to chat. At last he passed the sleeping hare and saw the goal ahead. His legs were very tired now, but he hurried on as fast as he could.

Just as the tortoise reached the goal, the hare woke up. He jumped up and ran down the road, pell-mell, hippety-hop, but he was too late. The tortoise had reached the goal before him.

The hare hung his head in shame.

"Slow and steady wins the race," said the fox.

The Wise Man of Gotham

THERE was once a man of Gotham who was going to the market at Nottingham to sell cheese. As he was going down the hill to Nottingham Bridge, one of his cheeses fell out of his basket and rolled down the hill.

"Ah, there!" said the man. "Can you run to market alone? In that case, I'll send one after another after you." He put down his basket and took out the cheeses and rolled them down the hill. Some went into one bush, and some went into another.

"I want all of you to meet me in the market place," he said. And when he came to the market to meet his cheeses, he stayed there until it was almost time to go home. Then he went about to ask of his friends and neighbors, and other men, if they had seen his cheeses come to market.

"Who would bring them?" asked one of the market men.

"Why, themselves!" said the fellow. "They know the way well enough." But after more time passed, and they still did not appear, the man declared, "I was afraid, seeing them run so fast, that they would run beyond the market. They must now be almost at York."

Thereupon he hired a horse to ride to York, to see if his cheeses were there. But to this day, no man can tell him where they are.

The Two Frogs

ALL SUMMER long there had been no rain, and all the lakes and streams had dried up. Two frogs, looking for water, came upon a deep well. They sat down and argued as to whether they should dive in or not.

Said one frog: "The water down there looks so good! I think we should jump in. We'll have plenty of fresh water if we do, and we'll have it all to ourselves, besides."

The second frog shook his head, and turned away from the well.

"What you say may be true," he said, "but suppose this well dries up, too? Then where will we be—no water and no way to get out of the well."

The first frog thought for awhile. Then he, too, turned away from the well.

"You are right," he said. "It's always wise to think twice before you leap."

The Real Princess

ONCE upon a time there was a prince who wanted to marry a princess, but he wanted to be certain that she was a REAL princess. He traveled all over the world searching, searching. There were lots of princesses, but he never could be sure that they were REAL princesses. There was always something that didn't seem quite right.

At last he came home, feeling very sad, for he was afraid he never would find one to suit him.

One evening a terrible storm came up. The night was filled with lightning and the roar of thunder, and the rain streamed down. Suddenly there was a knocking at the gate, and the old king went out to open it.

It was a princess who stood outside. But what a state she was in! Water dripped from her hair and clothes; it ran in at the tops of her shoes and out at her heels. And yet she said that she was a real princess.

"Well, we shall soon find out whether she is or not," thought the queen.

She said nothing, however, but slipped into the bed chamber for royal guests, took off all the bedding, and put a pea on the bedstead. Then she piled twenty mattresses on top of the pea, and twenty eider-down featherbeds upon the mattresses. This was to be the princess's bed for the night.

In the morning the queen asked her how she had slept.

"Oh, miserably!" answered the princess. "I scarcely closed my eyes all night. Goodness only knows what was in my bed. I lay upon something terribly hard, so that I'm black and blue all over!"

"Here's your REAL princess!" the queen said to her son. "No one but a real princess is sensitive enough to feel a pea through twenty mattresses and twenty eider-down featherbeds."

So the prince joyfully asked her to be his wife, and they were married. And the pea was placed in the royal museum, where you may see it to this day, unless someone has stolen it.

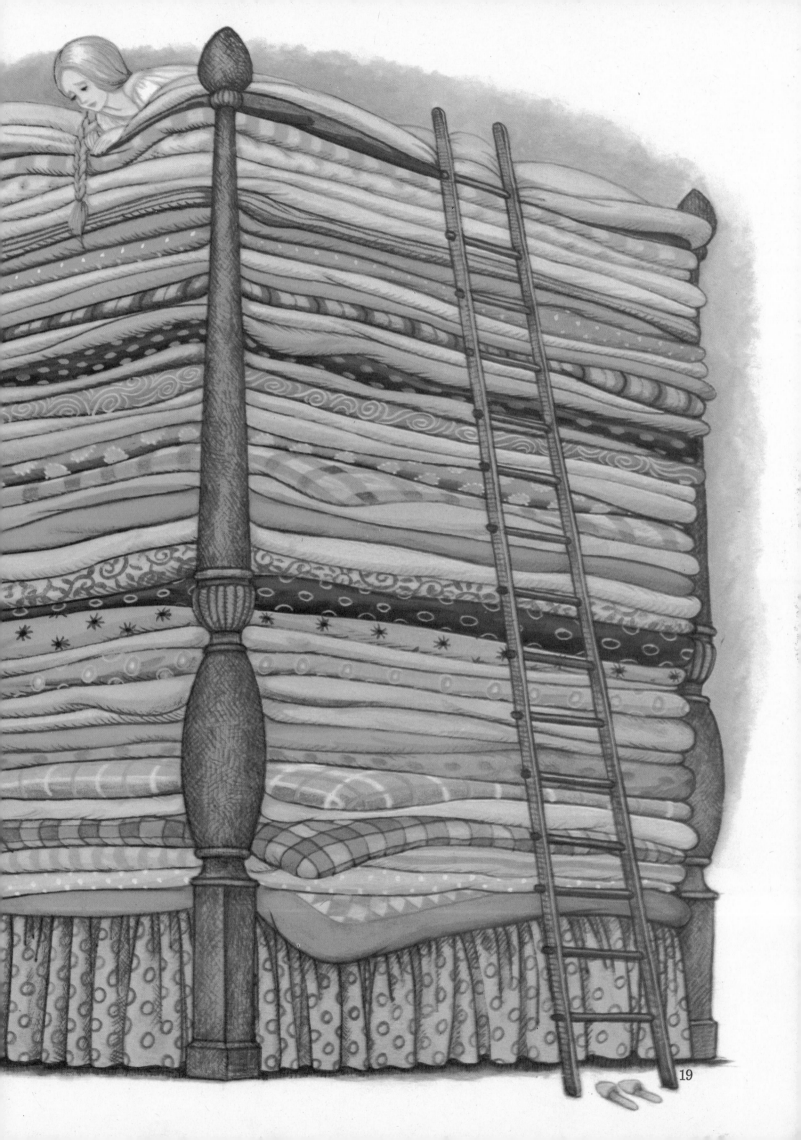

Little Eva

"OH, DEAR ME," sighed little Eva one fine morning. "I am tired of being a little girl. I wish I could be something else."

"Well," said a voice near her, "what would you like to be?"

Eva looked about in surprise. She saw no one, but the voice repeated the words, "What would you like to be?"

Just to see what would happen, Eva spoke up and said, "I would like to be a rosebud."

The words were hardly out of her mouth before she felt her skirt twisting close around her body in a very queer way. When she touched it, she found it was not cloth any longer — it was made of rose-leaves. She looked down at her feet. They seemed to be turning green, and her legs had funny little sharp things on them.

The next moment Eva knew she was a rosebud. She was growing on a bush in the garden. The wind swayed her gently back and forth. It was charming. Although she was a rosebud, she knew everything that went on around her. Suddenly she saw a lovely fairy bending over her.

"Ah," said the fairy, "this rose-petal is filled with dew. First I will drink the dew, then I will eat the tender end of the bud for breakfast."

"Don't, don't!" cried Eva. "If you do, you will eat my head."

"I won't eat that worm," she cried. "I'm not a real bird! I'm a—I'm a—" Just then the sky grew dark. The wind blew fiercely. Eva put her hands to her head, frightened, yet glad to find that she had hands and head, that she was not a bird.

"Why, it's raining hard," she said. "Where have I been? I must have fallen asleep under the apple tree." And then Eva ran into the house as fast as she could go, to tell her strange dream to her mother.

"And, oh, Mother," she cried, "I've decided that I would rather be a little girl than ANYTHING ELSE in the world!"

The fairy began to laugh.

"Please make me something else, quick," cried Eva. "Change me into a bird."

Before Eva knew how it happened, she was hopping about among the daisies as a bird.

"This is great fun," she cried, "but I'm hungry."

"Oh?" said a voice beside her. "Then I'll feed you."

In front of her stood a tiny elf, holding a worm in his hand.

Eva looked round, hoping to see a friendly face, but the only faces she saw were those of some green apples in a tree.

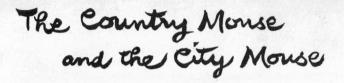

The Country Mouse and the City Mouse

ONCE there was a little country mouse who lived in the corner of a farmer's field. He was a very happy mouse. He always had enough to eat, and although it was simple fare—bits of grain and nuts and dried peas from the fields, and crumbs from the farmer's table — it suited him perfectly and he wanted nothing more.

One day, the little country mouse invited a city mouse to come and spend a few days with him.

"The country air and the peace and quiet will do you a world of good, cousin," he said.

So, in due time, the city mouse arrived. The country mouse welcomed his friend with open arms, and he brought out all the good things he had stored away to please his city-bred guest.

But the city mouse turned up his nose in scorn at such simple food. "My poor cousin!" he cried. "Is this all you have to eat? You really must come home with me and see how I live. Believe me, country life cannot compare with life in the city!"

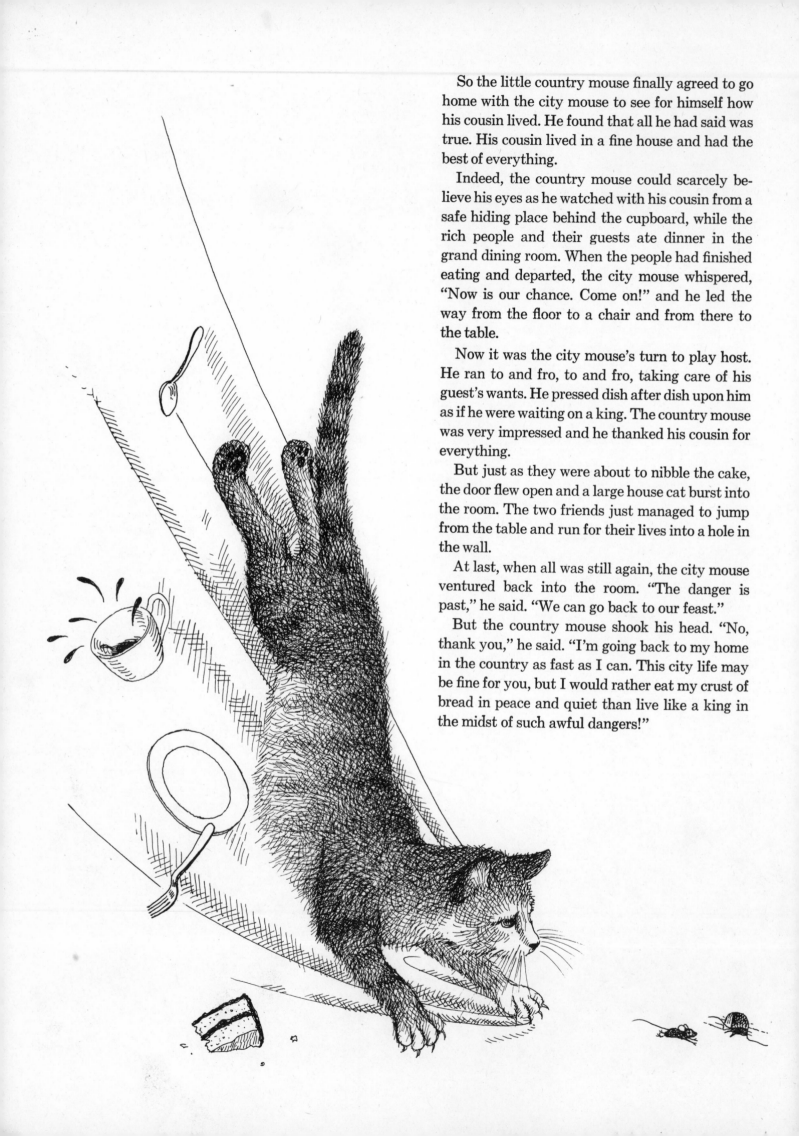

So the little country mouse finally agreed to go home with the city mouse to see for himself how his cousin lived. He found that all he had said was true. His cousin lived in a fine house and had the best of everything.

Indeed, the country mouse could scarcely believe his eyes as he watched with his cousin from a safe hiding place behind the cupboard, while the rich people and their guests ate dinner in the grand dining room. When the people had finished eating and departed, the city mouse whispered, "Now is our chance. Come on!" and he led the way from the floor to a chair and from there to the table.

Now it was the city mouse's turn to play host. He ran to and fro, to and fro, taking care of his guest's wants. He pressed dish after dish upon him as if he were waiting on a king. The country mouse was very impressed and he thanked his cousin for everything.

But just as they were about to nibble the cake, the door flew open and a large house cat burst into the room. The two friends just managed to jump from the table and run for their lives into a hole in the wall.

At last, when all was still again, the city mouse ventured back into the room. "The danger is past," he said. "We can go back to our feast."

But the country mouse shook his head. "No, thank you," he said. "I'm going back to my home in the country as fast as I can. This city life may be fine for you, but I would rather eat my crust of bread in peace and quiet than live like a king in the midst of such awful dangers!"

The Gnat and the Bull

ONCE there was a silly gnat who kept buzzing about the head of a bull. Finally he settled down on one of the bull's horns.

"Pardon me, Mr. Bull," he said, "if I am disturbing you. If you find my weight a burden to you, just say so, and I will be off in a moment."

"Do not give it another thought," replied the bull. "It is all the same to me whether you go or stay. To tell you the truth, I did not even know you were there."

And as the gnat, his feelings hurt, flew away, the bull shook his head. "It takes a small mind," he said, "to be so conceited!"

The Golden Eggs

ONE DAY a farmer went to the nest of his goose to see if she had laid an egg. To his surprise, he found, instead of an ordinary goose egg, an egg of solid gold.

"What a fine goose!" he cried. "I can sell this egg for a great deal of money."

Every morning after that the farmer found another golden egg in the nest. Every day he sold the golden egg. He was slowly growing rich.

But as the farmer grew rich, he grew greedy.

One day he said to himself, "My goose lays just one golden egg each day. No doubt there are many more inside her!" And he had no rest until he had killed the goose.

But when he looked inside the bird, there were no golden eggs at all! It was just the same as any other goose.

"Oh, me, oh, my!" said the farmer. "Why was I so greedy? Now I shall be poor again. I have killed the goose that laid the golden eggs!"

The Little Red Hen

Once upon a time, a pig, a duck, a cat, and a little red hen all lived together in a cozy little house on a pretty green hill.

All day long, the pig wallowed happily in his juicy mud puddle, the duck swam happily on her little pond, and the cat slept happily in the sun. This left all the work of the house for the little red hen to do.

One day as the little red hen was scratching about in the yard, looking for a nice beetle for her

dinner, she came upon a grain of wheat. It gave her an idea.

"Who will plant this grain of wheat?" she called.

"Not I," grunted the pig from the middle of his puddle.

"Not I," quacked the duck from her pond.

"Not I," purred the cat from her place in the sun.

"Then I will," said the little red hen.
And she did.

The grain of wheat sprouted, and it grew and grew until it was tall and golden and ready to be cut.

"Who will cut the wheat?" called the little red hen.

"Not I," grunted the pig from the middle of his puddle.

"Not I," quacked the duck from her pond.

"Not I," purred the cat from her place in the sun.

"Then I will," said the little red hen.
And she did.

When the wheat was cut and ready to be ground into flour, the little red hen called, "Who will take the wheat to the mill?"

"Not I," grunted the pig from the middle of his puddle.

"Not I," quacked the duck from her pond.

"Not I," purred the cat from her place in the sun.

"Then I will," said the little red hen.
And she did.

Soon a little sack of fine flour came back from the mill.

"Who will make the flour into bread?" called the little red hen.

"Not I," grunted the pig from the middle of his puddle.

"Not I," quacked the duck from her pond.

"Not I," purred the cat from her place in the sun.

"Then I will," said the little red hen.
And she did.

When the bread was baked, the little red hen took it from the oven. It was the most beautiful crusty brown loaf she had ever seen.

"Who will eat the bread?" she called.

"I will!" grunted the pig, and he scrambled out of his puddle.

"I will!" quacked the duck, and she paddled in from her pond.

"I will!" purred the cat, and she jumped up from her place in the sun.

"Oh, no, you won't," said the little red hen. "I found the grain of wheat. I planted it. I reaped the ripe grain. I took it to the mill. I baked the bread. I shall eat it myself."

And she did.

Cinderella

ONCE there was a girl who was as good as she was beautiful. She lived with her stepmother and two stepsisters who were ugly and cruel. They made her do all the hard work, scrubbing and cleaning and tending the fire. At night she sat in the chimney corner to rest. Her ragged clothes were always covered with cinders and ashes and so she was called Cinderella.

One day the king's son announced that he was going to give a ball. The stepmother and the stepsisters were invited and they bought fine clothes for themselves. But they told Cinderella that she could not go to the ball. Cinderella worked harder than ever to help her stepmother and sisters dress for the ball. But in spite of their fine clothes and feathers, they could not hide their ugliness.

When they left for the ball, Cinderella was so unhappy that she began to cry. Suddenly a fairy godmother appeared. "My child," she said, "you, too, shall go to the ball." She touched Cinderella with her wand and the rags fell away. Cinderella was dressed in a beautiful ball gown, with jewels in her hair, and she wore a lovely pair of glass slippers on her feet.

Then the fairy godmother waved her wand and made a fine carriage out of a pumpkin. She made eight horses out of mice to drive the carriage. She made a coachman out of a rat, and six footmen out of lizards. When she had finished her magic work, Cinderella was as splendid as any princess.

"But you must be home by midnight!" said the

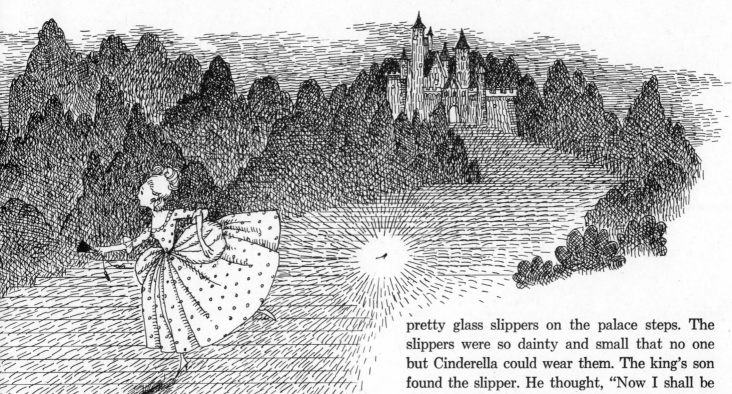

pretty glass slippers on the palace steps. The slippers were so dainty and small that no one but Cinderella could wear them. The king's son found the slipper. He thought, "Now I shall be able to find the lovely girl who ran away so quickly." He sent his messengers to find the girl whose foot fitted the slipper.

All the fine ladies of the court tried on the slipper. But it did not fit any of them. Then

fairy godmother. "The magic will end at twelve o'clock and after that you will be all in rags again."

Cinderella was the most beautiful girl at the ball. Everyone talked about her and wondered who she was. Even her stepmother and stepsisters did not recognize her. The king's son danced with her all night and fell in love with her. Cinderella was so happy that she forgot about the time.

Suddenly the clock struck the first notes of twelve. Cinderella knew that she must hurry away from the palace. But even before she got back to her chimney corner, everything had disappeared and she was again dressed all in rags.

In her haste, Cinderella had lost one of her

Cinderella's stepmother and sisters tried the slipper on. But it did not fit them either. At last one of the messengers saw Cinderella hiding in her corner. He asked her to try on the slipper.

The slipper fitted Cinderella perfectly! Then Cinderella pulled the other slipper out of her pocket and put it on. Now everyone knew who the lovely girl at the ball had been.

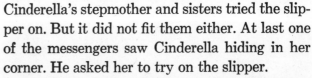

Cinderella was taken to the palace where she married the king's son.
And they lived happily ever after.

The Golden Touch

ONCE upon a time, there lived a king named Midas. Although this king had a good wife and a little daughter whom he loved very much, there was something he seemed to love much more dearly—and that was gold.

Each day he went into his countinghouse, where he counted stacks of golden coins again and again. It was his greatest pleasure in life, and he dreamed only of getting more golden coins to count.

While he was counting one day, he heard a mysterious voice say, "I have come to grant you whatever you wish for most."

King Midas did not hesitate very long. "I wish," he said, "that everything I touch would turn to gold."

"You have your wish," said the voice.

King Midas was overjoyed, thinking of all the gold that would now be his. He picked up a pebble. It turned to gold. He touched every flower he could find in the garden and they turned to gold. "What a wonderful gift!" he exclaimed.

Some time later, he sat down to eat. As he pulled the chair away from the table, it turned to gold. He reached out for some food, but to his mounting alarm, he discovered that the meat, the bread, the fruit—everything—turned into solid gold at his touch. It could not be eaten. Midas became frightened. Now he began to wonder how

he would live with nothing to eat.

He walked out into the garden to think. Just then his little daughter ran up to him and gave him a hug. Midas bent down to kiss her—and SHE turned into gold!

As Midas gazed at his only daughter, now only no more than a golden statue, he realized how foolish he had been to love money for its own sake. He cried bitter tears. At last the same voice he had heard before said to him, "Go down to the river, wash your hands, and your golden touch will be gone. Then fill a pitcher with water from the river and sprinkle it over everything you have already turned into gold."

King Midas hurried along to do as he had been told. When the river water was sprinkled on the golden statue of his child, the little girl returned to life. The flowers returned to their natural color and beauty. Food could again be taken in hand without turning hard and shining yellow.

King Midas had learned his lesson. He no longer yearned for gold above all other things in the world.

The Ugly Duckling

THE COUNTRY was lovely just then—it was summer. In a sunny spot stood an old mansion surrounded by a deep lake. Large green leaves grew from the walls of the house down to the water's edge.

In among the leaves it was as secluded as in the depth of a forest. There a duck was sitting on her nest. She was tired of sitting, for it had been such a long time. But at last her ducklings were about to be hatched.

One egg after another began to crack. All the chicks were poking their heads out. "Cheep, cheep!" they said. "How big the world is!"

"I suppose you are all here now," said their mother, looking about. "No, that big egg is still uncracked." Sighing, she settled herself on the nest again.

At last the big egg cracked and the young one came tumbling out. The mother duck stared at him. "What a strange, big duckling!" she said. None of the others look like that. Can he be a turkey duck? Well, we'll soon find out. Into the water he shall go, if I have to push him in myself."

The next day was sunny and fine, and the mother duck went down to the lake with her family.

Splash! Into the water she sprang. "Quack, quack!" she said, and one duckling after another plumped into the water after her. They floated beautifully. Even the big ugly gray one swam about with them.

Then they went to the duck yard. The other ducks stared at them and said, "Look, here's another tribe—as if there weren't enough of us already! And how ugly that duckling is! We won't stand for him!" And one duck flew at him and bit him on the neck.

"Leave him alone," said the mother duck. "He isn't doing any harm."

But the poor ugly duckling was made fun of by all the other ducks, and by the chickens, too. "He's so big and ugly," they all said. And the ducks bit him, and the hens pecked him. Even his brothers and sisters were unkind to him. He did not know what to do or where to go. He ran through the hedge, and the birds in the bushes flew away.

"They are afraid of me because I am so ugly," he thought, and he ran on. At last he came to a broad marsh, where the wild ducks lived. There he lay the whole night, too weary to move.

In the morning the wild ducks flew up to have a look at their new companion. The little duckling bowed.

"You are really very ugly," they said, "but we don't care as long as you do not wish to marry into our family."

Poor duckling! He certainly never thought of marriage. All he wanted was to be allowed to lie among the reeds and drink the water from the marsh.

"I think I will go out into the wide world," he said. And he bid the wild ducks goodby and went on his way. Soon he found some water to swim and dive in, but he was slighted by every living creature because of his ugliness.

Now autumn came. The leaves in the wood turned yellow and brown. One evening, when the sun was just setting, a flock of beautiful large birds appeared out of the bushes. The ugly duckling had never seen anything so beautiful. They were dazzling white, with long, curving necks. They were swans. The duckling felt drawn to them, though he did not know why. Then, uttering a strange cry, the swans spread their broad, white wings and flew away to warmer lands for the winter.

It would be too sad to tell about all the misery the ugly duckling had to bear during the hard winter. But at last the sun began to shine warmly again. It found the duckling in the marsh, among the rushes.

Then all at once he raised his wings and they flapped with much greater strength than ever before, and they bore him off. Before he knew it, he found himself in a large garden. Just in front of him were three beautiful swans. The duckling recognized them and he was filled with a strange sadness.

"I will fly to them and let them hack me to pieces," he thought, "because one as ugly as I dares to come near them. But I don't care. Better to die than go on suffering so much misery."

So he flew into the water and swam toward the stately swans.

"Kill me!" he cried, and he bowed his head toward the water and waited for death. But what did he see reflected in the clear water?

He saw below him his own image, but he was no longer a clumsy dark gray bird, ugly and ungainly. He was a swan!

The big swans swam round and round him and stroked him with their bills.

Some little children came into the garden, and the smallest one cried out, "There is a new one!" The other children shouted with joy, "Yes, a new swan has come!" And one and all said, "The new one is the prettiest of them all!"

The new swan felt quite shy, and hid his head under his wing. He was very happy, but not at all proud, for a good heart never becomes proud. He thought of how he had been pursued and scorned. And now he heard them all say that he was the most beautiful of all beautiful birds! He rustled his feathers and said, "I never dreamed there could be so much happiness when I was the Ugly Duckling!"

The Three Little Pigs

ONCE there were three little pigs who went out into the world to seek their fortunes. Each little pig took a different road.

Soon the first little pig met a man with a load of straw. "Please, may I have some straw to build a house?" asked the little pig. And the man gave him some straw.

The first little pig had just finished his house when a big, bad wolf came along. "Little pig, little pig, let me come in," said the wolf.

"No, no, by the hair on my chinny-chin-chin," said the little pig.

"Then I'll huff and I'll puff and I'll blow your house in!" cried the wolf. So he huffed and he puffed and he blew the house in.

The second little pig met a man with a bundle of twigs. "Please, may I have some twigs to build a house?" asked the little pig. And the man gave him some twigs.

But no sooner had the second little pig finished his house than the big, bad wolf came to call. "Little pig, little pig, let me come in," said the wolf.

"No, no, by the hair on my chinny-chin-chin," said the little pig.

"Then I'll huff and I'll puff and I'll blow your house in!" cried the wolf. So he huffed and he puffed, and he puffed and he huffed, and he blew the house in.

Now the third little pig met a man with a wheelbarrow full of bricks. "Please, may I have some bricks to build a house?" asked the little pig. And the man gave him some bricks.

But no sooner had the third little pig finished his house than the big, bad wolf came along. "Little pig, little pig, let me come in!" he cried.

"No, no, by the hair on my chinny-chin-chin," said the little pig.

"Then I'll huff and I'll puff and I'll blow your house in!" cried the wolf. So he huffed and he puffed, and he puffed and he huffed, and he huffed and he puffed again. But he could not blow the house in.

The wolf was very angry and thought to himself, "I must catch that little pig." So he said, "There are some nice fat turnips in Farmer Brown's field. Will you go with me to get some at six o'clock tomorrow morning, little pig?"

"Yes, I will," said the little pig. But he got up at five o'clock and was home cooking his turnips when the wolf came to call for him.

The big, bad wolf was very, very angry. But he thought of another way to catch the little pig. "I know where there is a fine red-apple tree. Will you go with me at five o'clock tomorrow morning to pick some apples?"

"Yes, I will," said the little pig. But the little pig went for the apples at four o'clock. He had not started early enough, however, and he was still up in the tree when the wolf came along.

"Are the apples sweet?" asked the wolf.

"Yes," said the little pig. "I will throw you one." So he threw an apple as far as he could, and while the wolf went to get it, the little pig climbed down the tree and ran home.

Early the next morning the wolf hurried to the little pig's house. He HAD to catch that pig! So he climbed up on the roof and slid down the chimney. But the little pig had seen him coming, and took the lid off a large kettle of water which was on the fire. There was a great big splash! And that was the end of the big, bad wolf.

The Dragon and the Monkey

ONCE upon a time, in the great China Sea, there lived a dragon and his wife. Now this dragon loved his wife dearly, and he did everything in his power to grant her every wish.

One day he noticed that his wife looked pale and unhappy.

"What is the matter, my sweet?" he asked. "You look so troubled."

"I can't tell you," his wife said. "It won't do any good, for I know that you cannot get me what I want."

"Have I ever failed to get you what you wanted?" he asked, giving her a hurt look.

And he coaxed so hard that at last she said, "I have been told that monkeys' hearts are a most delicious dish. I long to eat one. If I don't, I think I shall die."

The dragon could not even bear the thought of losing his wife, but how would he ever get a monkey's heart?

"Monkeys live high in the trees," he said. "How could I ever catch one?"

His wife began to cry. "You see, you didn't mean it when you said you'd do anything for me! Oh, I shall surely die now!"

The dragon thought and thought about what he should do. At last he said to himself, "Well, it can't hurt to try." So he left the sea, went ashore, and journeyed until he came to a jungle. There, at the top of a tall tree, he spied a monkey.

"Good day, you pretty thing," said the dragon in his sweetest voice. "That is such a tall tree you're in. Aren't you afraid you'll fall out?"

The monkey burst out laughing. "Ha, ha, ha!" he laughed. "Who ever heard of a monkey falling out of a tree!"

The dragon tried again.

"That isn't a very good tree," he said. " I know a place full of trees laden with wonderful, juicy fruit. It's not far from here—just across the sea."

"What a foolish dragon you are!" said the monkey. "What you say is no doubt true, but how would I cross the sea?"

"That is easy," replied the dragon with a sweet smile. "Just jump on my back, hold on tight, and I'll swim across with you."

So the little monkey came down and climbed up on the dragon's back. The dragon, of course, lost no time getting back to the China Sea. When they were halfway across, the dragon suddenly dived down beneath the surface of the water.

"Where are you going?" cried the monkey in alarm.

"I might as well tell you now," said the dragon. "There is no forest, no trees, and no juicy fruit.

My wife, who is ill, must have a monkey's heart —nothing else will cure her. So I am trying to drown you to get your heart for my wife."

The monkey had to think fast. "My poor friend," he said, "why didn't you tell me all this before we started out? I would be happy to give up my heart to help your wife. But don't you know that monkeys never carry their hearts around with them? I left mine in the tree where you found me. Of course, if you don't mind going back, I'll be glad to fetch it for you."

The dragon turned around and went back to the jungle, to the very tree where he first saw the monkey. The little monkey took a great leap and a bound, and was safe again in the topmost branch. The dragon waited and waited, and begged and begged the monkey to come down with his heart. But the monkey didn't bother to answer him.

And, for all anyone knows, the foolish dragon is still waiting there. Perhaps the time will come when he will realize that monkeys not only carry their hearts with them, but their thinking caps, as well!

Do What You Can

ONCE there was a farmer who had a large field of corn. He plowed it and weeded it carefully, for he wanted to sell the corn and buy many things for his family with the money.

But after he had worked hard for many weeks, he saw the corn wither and droop. There was no rain and he began to worry that he would have no crop at all. Every morning he went out to the field and looked at the thirsty stalks and wished for the rain to fall.

One day, as the farmer stood looking up at the sky, two little raindrops saw him, and one said to the other, "Look at that farmer. He took such pains with his field of corn, and now it is drying up. I wish we could help him."

"Yes," said the other, "but you are only a little raindrop. What can you do? You can't wet even one hill."

"To be sure," said the first, "I cannot do much. But perhaps I can cheer the farmer a little and I am going to do what I can. Here I go!"

The first raindrop had no sooner started for the field than the second one said, "Well, if you insist upon going, I think I will go, too. Here I come!" And down he went.

One raindrop fell—*pat*—on the farmer's nose. The second raindrop fell—*pat*—on a stalk of corn.

"Oh-ho!" said the farmer. "A raindrop! Where did it come from? I do believe we shall have a shower."

By this time a great many raindrops had come together to see what all the commotion was about. When they saw the two kind little raindrops falling down to cheer the farmer and water his corn, one said, "If you two are going on such a good errand, I'll go, too!" And down HE came.

"And I!" said another.

"And I!"

And so said they all, until a whole shower came and the corn was watered. Then the corn grew and ripened . . . all because one little raindrop tried to do what it could.

The Fir Tree

FAR AWAY in the forest stood a pretty little fir tree. The warm sun shone on it, the fresh breeze blew about it, but the fir tree was not happy. All around it were tall pines and firs, and the little fir tree wanted to be like them. So it did not heed the sunlight or the air that fluttered its leaves, or even the children who passed by, prattling happily.

Each year, the little fir tree grew taller, and as it grew it complained because it was not as tall as the other trees. Two winters passed, and when the third came, the tree had grown so tall that the hare was obliged to run around it.

In the autumn, the woodcutters always came and cut down several of the tallest trees, and the young fir, which had now grown quite tall, shuddered as the noble trees fell to the ground with a crash. Then the trees were placed one on another on wagons, and dragged by horses out of the forest. Where were they going? the fir tree wondered. What would become of them?

The swallows did not know, but the stork thought they were used to make the masts of sailing ships.

"Oh, how I wish I were tall enough to go to sea!" said the fir tree.

"Rejoice that you are young," said the sunbeam. And the wind kissed the tree, and the dew wept tears over it. But the fir tree did not understand.

A short time before the next Christmas, the fir tree was the first to fall. As the axe cut sharply into its trunk, it fell to the ground with a groan, conscious only of pain and faintness. Nor was the journey at all pleasant. Then the tree felt itself being unloaded with several other trees, in the courtyard of a house. It heard a man say, "We want only one and this one is the prettiest."

Then the tree was carried into a beautiful big room, and placed in a large tub full of sand. The tub was covered with a cloth and placed on a rich carpet. How the tree trembled! What was going to happen to it now? Some young girls came, and the servants helped them to trim the tree with lovely ornaments. And at the very top they fastened a glittering star made of gold tinsel. Oh, it was truly beautiful!

And now the doors were thrown open and a group of children rushed in. Behind them came the older people. For a moment the children stood silent with delight, and then they shouted for joy and danced merrily around the tree, snatching off one present after another.

"What are they doing?" thought the tree. "What will happen next?"

In the morning, the servants came in and dragged the fir tree out of the room and upstairs to the attic. They threw it on the floor in a dark corner where no daylight shone, and there they left it. "What does this mean?" thought the tree. "Why did they leave me here in the dark?" and it leaned against the wall and thought and thought.

"It is winter now in the forest," thought the tree. "The ground is hard and covered with snow. That is why the people haven't planted me yet. That is why I am left here under cover until spring comes. But I wish it weren't so dark and so terribly lonely, with not even a hare for company. How pleasant it was in the forest, when the hare would run by—and jump over me, too! But I didn't like it then. Oh, it is so lonely here!"

"Squeak! Squeak!" said a little mouse, stealing out of his hole and creeping toward the tree. Then another came, and they both sniffed at the fir tree and crept in and out among the branches.

"Oh, it's so cold!" said a little mouse. "If it weren't, it would be quite comfortable here, eh, old fir tree?"

"I am not old," replied the fir tree. "There are many much older than I." And then the tree told the mice all about its youth. The mice had never heard anything like it before. "How much you have seen!" they said. "How happy you have been!"

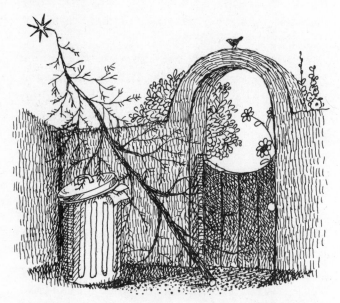

One morning people came and pulled the tree out of the corner and threw it roughly on the floor; then the servants dragged it out to the stairs, and it saw the daylight again.

"Now life is beginning again," thought the tree, rejoicing in the sunshine and fresh air.

It was carried downstairs and out into the yard so quickly that it forgot to look at itself, but gazed about, for there was much to see. The yard opened into a garden where flowers bloomed; the linden trees were in blossom; and swallows flew here and there, calling for their mates.

"Now I shall live," thought the tree, stretching its branches. But, alas! they were all withered and yellow, and it was lying in a corner among weeds and nettles. Then the tree looked at itself, and wished it had been left in the dark garret.

"Past! Past!" said the poor tree. "Oh, if only I had enjoyed myself while I could! Now it is too late—it is all past."

Then a boy came and chopped the tree into small pieces. The pieces were placed in a fire, where they blazed up brightly, and the tree sighed so deeply that each sigh was like a pistol shot. And at each explosion, which was a deep sigh, the tree thought of a summer day in the woods, or of a winter night there, when the stars were bright in the sky. And then the tree was burned.

The children played in the garden, and the youngest had on his shirt the golden star which the tree had worn on its happiest evening. Now that was past, the tree's life was past—and this story is past, as well.

The Sun and the Wind

ONE DAY, the sun and the wind had a quarrel. The wind said, "I am stronger than you." "No," said the sun, "I am stronger than you."

While they were arguing, they saw a traveler coming along the road. He wore a heavy coat, for the weather was cold.

"See that man?" said the wind. "Let us see which of us can make him take off his coat. The one who can do it is the stronger."

"Agreed," said the sun. "You may begin."

The wind blew and blew and blew. But the traveler only drew his coat closer about him. The wind blew even more fiercely. The trees rocked, the dust flew, but the traveler turned up his coat to protect his ears.

"What a gale this is!" he cried.

Now it was the sun's turn. He shone and shone. "How the weather has changed!" said the trav-

eler, and he unbuttoned his coat.

Still the sun shone, and soon the traveler was wiping the moisture from his face.

"This coat is too much for me," he said. "I will have to carry it." He took off his coat.

"You see?" said the sun. "I have won. I am the stronger."

"Wait a moment," replied the wind. "It is my turn again." And he blew and blew, and the air turned colder and colder.

"Crazy weather!" grumbled the traveler. He put his coat on again.

"There, you see!" cried the wind. "You made the man take off his coat, true. But I made him put it on again."

The sun laughed. "We are equally strong," he said. "I in my way, you in yours." And they never quarrelled again.

Rumpelstiltskin

THERE WAS once a poor miller who had a beautiful daughter. One day, it happened that he came to speak to the king and, to give himself importance, he said, "I have a daughter who can spin straw into gold."

The king did not believe this, of course, but he had the girl brought to him. He led her to a room full of straw, gave her a wheel and spindle, and said, "Get to work. Spin this straw into gold by morning, or you shall die." Then he locked the door behind him.

The poor girl sat down and burst into tears. She had no way to spin straw into gold—how could she? Suddenly, the door opened and a little man came in. "Good evening, my pretty one," he said. "Why are you weeping?"

The girl explained, and the dwarf said, "What will you give me if I do it for you?"

"My scarf," said the girl.

He took the scarf, sat down before the wheel, and *grind, grind, grind*—three times did he grind—and the spindle was full. Then he put another thread in, and *grind, grind, grind*, the second was full. So he spun on until morning, when all the straw was spun and all the spindles were full of gold.

The king arrived at sunrise. He was astonished and delighted at the sight of all the gold, but it only made him greedy for more. He put the girl into a larger room full of straw, and ordered her to spin it all in one night, or die.

Once more, the girl sat down to weep, and once more the door opened and the dwarf appeared. This time she offered him her ring if he would spin the straw into gold. The little man took the ring, began to turn the wheel, and by morning all the straw had turned to shining gold.

The king was overjoyed, but he was still not satisfied. He put the girl into an even larger room full of straw, and said, "Spin this into gold tonight and tomorrow you shall be my wife."

As soon as the girl was alone, the dwarf appeared for the third time. "What will you give me if I spin all this straw for you?" he asked.

"I have nothing more to give you," she told him.

"Then promise, if you become queen, to give me your first child."

"Who knows how things may turn out between then and now?" thought the girl, and she promised to do as he asked. At once, the little man sat down to spin the straw into gold.

In the morning, when the king saw that his orders had been obeyed, he took the miller's daughter to be his queen.

After a year had passed, a beautiful baby boy was born to the king and queen. The little man was forgotten, till one day he suddenly walked into the queen's chamber, and said, "Give me what you promised me."

The queen was frightened. She offered the dwarf all the riches of the kingdom if he would only let her keep the child.

"No!" he answered. "I want what you promised me!"

Then the queen began to weep so bitterly that the little man took pity on her and said, "I will give you three days. If in that time you can find out my name, you may keep the child."

All night long the queen tried to recall every name she had ever heard, and sent a messenger to learn what names were usually given to people in that country. When, next day, the dwarf came again, she began with Algernon, Balthazar, Caspar, and went on to all the other names she knew or had heard of. But always the dwarf said, "That is not my name."

The third day, the messenger came back and said, "I have not been able to find a single new name, but as I came over the mountains, I saw a little hut in the woods, and near the hut burned a little fire, and round the fire danced a funny little man, who hopped upon one leg, and sang:

"Today I brew, tomorrow I bake,
Next day the queen's child I'll take;
How glad I am that nobody knows
My name is Rumpelstiltskin!"

How happy the queen was at hearing this! And when the dwarf came again and said, "Queen, have you guessed my name?" the queen said mischievously, "Is it Ichabod?"

"No."

"Is it Carl?"

"No."

"Well, then, can your name be Rumpelstiltskin?"

At this, the dwarf flew into a terrible rage. He jumped up and down and screamed, so angry was he. Then he turned and rushed from the room and was never seen again.

The Ant and the Grasshopper

ONE FROSTY autumn day, an ant was busily storing away some kernels of wheat that he had gathered during the summer to tide him over the coming winter.

A grasshopper, half-dead from hunger, came limping by. When he saw what the ant was doing, he begged for a morsel from the ant's store to save his life.

"What were you doing all summer while I was busy harvesting?" asked the ant.

"Oh," replied the grasshopper, "I was not idle. I was singing lovely songs all day long."

"Well," said the ant grimly, "since you sang all summer, it looks as though you will have to dance all winter."

Then, as he was closing the door on the grasshopper's sad face, the ant remembered how much he had enjoyed the grasshopper's singing all summer, and he opened his door again.

"You may come in and dine with me," he said. "But I hope you have learned your lesson—always prepare today for tomorrow's needs!"

The Crow and the Pitcher

A CROW, so thirsty that he could not even say, "Caw-caw!" came upon a pitcher which had once been full of water. But when he put his beak into the pitcher's mouth, he found that only a little bit of water was left at the bottom, and try as he might, he could not reach far enough into the pitcher to reach the water.

Just as he was about to give up, a thought came to him. He picked up a pebble and dropped it into the pitcher. Then he picked up another pebble and dropped that into the pitcher. One by one, he kept dropping pebbles into the pitcher until the water reached the brim. Then he perched himself upon the handle and drank until his thirst was quenched.

"Where there's a will," he said to himself, "there's always a way."

Goldilocks and the Three Bears

THERE were once three bears who lived in a little cottage in the woods. The father was a great, big, enormous bear; the mother was a medium, middle-sized bear; and the baby was a wee, tiny bear.

"Let's take a walk before breakfast," said Father Bear one morning.

"Very well," said Mother Bear. "We'll put our porridge on the table to cool."

But while they were gone, a little girl named Goldilocks came to their house. She had been playing in the woods, and when she saw the pretty house, she was curious. Pushing open the door, she walked in. It was just as pretty inside.

"Well, well!" she said to herself. "Breakfast is ready, and I am hungry."

Father Bear's porridge was in a great, big, enormous bowl. Goldilocks tasted it first. But it was too hot.

Next she tasted Mother Bear's porridge in the medium, middle-sized bowl. But it was too cold.

Then she saw Baby Bear's porridge in the wee, tiny bowl. It was just right, so Goldilocks ate it all up.

Next she tried out the chairs. The great, big enormous chair was too high. The medium, middle-sized chair was too deep. But the wee, tiny chair was just right. Goldilocks was so pleased that she plopped up and down on it, until *crack!* she broke the chair.

Then she went upstairs. She saw the beds of the three bears and, feeling tired, decided to take a nap.

First she lay down on the great, big bed, but it was too hard. Then she lay down on the middle-sized bed, but it was too soft. Finally she tried the wee, tiny bed, and it was so comfortable that she fell sound asleep.

Pretty soon the bears came home for their breakfast. But what was this? Spoons IN the bowls instead of BESIDE them!

"SOMEBODY'S BEEN TASTING MY POR-RIDGE," said Father Bear in his great, big, enormous voice.

"Somebody's been tasting MY porridge," said Mother Bear in her medium, middle-sized voice.

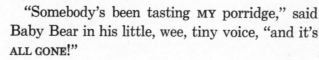

"Somebody's been tasting MY porridge," said Baby Bear in his little, wee, tiny voice, "and it's ALL GONE!"

Just then Father Bear noticed that the pillows on the chairs didn't look quite straight.

"SOMEBODY'S BEEN SITTING IN MY CHAIR!" he said in his great, big enormous voice.

"Somebody's been sitting in MY chair," said Mother Bear in her medium, middle-sized voice.

"Somebody's been sitting in MY chair," said Baby Bear in his wee, tiny voice, "and the bottom's fallen out of it!" He began to cry wee, tiny tears.

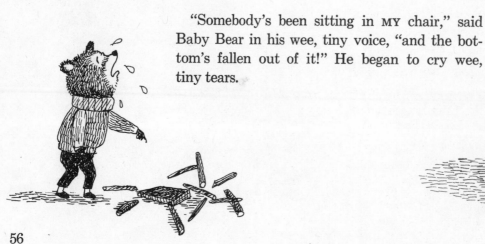

Then the three bears went upstairs.

"SOMEBODY'S BEEN LYING IN MY BED," said Father Bear in his great, big, enormous voice.

"Somebody's been lying in MY bed," said Mother Bear in her medium, middle-sized voice.

"Somebody's been lying in my bed, and here she is!" said Baby Bear in his wee, tiny voice.

When Goldilocks opened her eyes and saw the three bears staring at her, she was so startled that she jumped straight out of bed, raced down the stairs and out the front door, and she ran and ran until she got back home. And she hasn't been quite so curious about other people's houses since that day.

The Teeny-Tiny Woman

ONCE upon a time there was a teeny-tiny woman who lived in a teeny-tiny house in a teeny-tiny village. One day the teeny-tiny woman put on her teeny-tiny bonnet, and went out of her teeny-tiny house to take a teeny-tiny walk.

And when this teeny-tiny woman had gone a teeny-tiny way, she came to a teeny-tiny gate; so the teeny-tiny woman opened the teeny-tiny gate, and went into a teeny-tiny churchyard.

And when this teeny-tiny woman had got into the teeny-tiny churchyard, she saw a teeny-tiny bone on a teeny-tiny grave, and the teeny-tiny woman said to her teeny-tiny self, "This teeny-tiny bone will make some teeny-tiny soup for my teeny-tiny supper."

So the teeny-tiny woman put the teeny-tiny bone into her teeny-tiny pocket, and went to her teeny-tiny house.

Now, when the teeny-tiny woman got home to her teeny-tiny house, she was a teeny-tiny tired; so she went up her teeny-tiny stairs to her teeny-tiny bed,

and put the teeny-tiny bone into a teeny-tiny cupboard.

And when this teeny-tiny woman had been to sleep for a teeny-tiny time, she was awakened by a teeny-tiny voice from the teeny-tiny cupboard, which said, "Give me my bone!" And this teeny-tiny woman was a teeny-tiny frightened, so she hid her teeny-tiny head under the teeny-tiny clothes, and went to sleep again.

And when she had been to sleep again a teeny-tiny time, the teeny-tiny voice cried out from the teeny-tiny cupboard, a teeny-tiny louder, "Give me my bone!"

This made the teeny-tiny woman a teeny-tiny more frightened, so she hid her teeny-tiny head a teeny-tiny farther under the teeny-tiny clothes. And when the teeny-tiny woman had been to sleep again a teeny-tiny time, the teeny-tiny voice from the teeny-tiny cupboard said again, a teeny-tiny louder, "GIVE ME MY BONE!"

And this teeny-tiny woman was a teeny-tiny bit more frightened, but she put her teeny-tiny head out of the teeny-tiny clothes, and said in her loudest teeny-tiny voice, "TAKE IT!"

Jack and the Beanstalk

A LONG TIME AGO, a boy named Jack lived with his mother in a poor little house. One day his mother said, "Jack, we have no money left for food. Take the cow to the market in the village and sell her."

On the way, Jack met a strange old man. The man showed him five beans which he said were magic beans. "If you plant them," he told Jack, "they will grow right up to the sky." So Jack sold his mother's cow to the man for the beans.

When Jack got home, his mother said, "What! You sold our last cow for five beans?" She was so angry that she threw the beans out of the window and sent Jack to bed without any supper.

In the morning, Jack looked out of the window. The magic beans had sprouted! He saw a great beanstalk that reached all the way up to the sky. Jack decided to climb up the beanstalk to see what there was to see.

He climbed and climbed and climbed. When he got to the top, Jack started walking. The first thing he saw was a big house. A big woman was standing in the doorway.

"Good morning," said Jack. "I am very hungry. Could you please give me some breakfast?"

Now this woman was really the wife of a giant. She said to Jack, "Is it breakfast you want? 'Tis breakfast you will BE! Run away, before the giant comes home and eats you up!"

But Jack would not run away. Then the woman felt sorry for him and gave him a bowl of porridge. While he was eating it, they heard the giant coming home. His heavy footsteps made the whole house shake. Thump! THUMP! THUMP!

"Get into the oven, quick!" said the giant's wife. Jack jumped up and crawled into the oven. When the giant came into the house he roared, "Fee-fi-fo-fum! I smell a boy!" But his wife said, "There is nobody in the house. Eat your breakfast and take a nap."

After breakfast, the giant said to his wife, "Bring me my hen that lays golden eggs." The wife brought a big black hen with a shiny red comb. "Lay!" said the giant to the hen. And the hen laid a big golden egg. "Lay!" he said to the hen again. Once more the hen laid a golden egg.

Then the giant took his nap. As soon as Jack heard him snoring, he popped out of the oven. He seized the hen and ran home as fast as he could. When he got home, Jack gave the hen to his mother. After that they never lacked for food. Whenever they needed money for food, Jack's mother would tell the hen to lay a golden egg.

But after a while Jack began to wonder if he could find something else up in the sky. So one day he went back up the beanstalk. Up and up and up he went. When he got to the top, he started walking.

Jack came to the same house again and saw the same woman in the doorway. This time he did not ask for breakfast. He quietly slipped into the house and hid himself in a big copper pot. Soon he heard the giant coming home. Thump! THUMP! THUMP!

"Fe-fi-fo-fum!" roared the giant to his wife. "I smell a boy!" They both went to the oven and looked in, but Jack was not there. The wife said, "There is nobody here." So the giant sat down and ate his breakfast.

61

Then the giant said to his wife, "Bring me my magic harp." The wife brought him his harp. "Sing!" said the giant to the harp. And the harp began to play beautiful songs. The music soon put the giant to sleep.

As soon as he was asleep, Jack jumped out of the copper pot. He seized the harp and started to run home. But almost as soon as Jack touched the harp, it cried out, "Master! Master!" This woke the giant who began to run after Jack.

Jack ran and ran and ran. At last he reached the beanstalk. Down he went as fast as he could, but the giant was right behind him. Halfway down, Jack saw his mother in the back yard, cutting wood. He cried out, "Mother! Mother! Bring the axe."

His mother ran over with the axe. When Jack got to the bottom, he took the axe and chopped down the beanstalk. Bang! CRASH! Down came the beanstalk, giant and all. And even to this day there is a deep hole where he sank out of sight.

After that Jack and his mother lived very happily. They had the hen that laid golden eggs and the harp that played beautiful songs.

Why the Bear is Stumpy-tailed

ONE DAY in winter a bear met a fox, who was carrying a string of fish.

"That's a fine string of fish!" said the bear, hungrily. "Where did you get them?"

"I've been fishing," said the fox with a sly smile. "It's very easy and I'm sure you could catch some yourself."

"Really?" asked the bear. He thought of how good some fish would taste for supper. "Tell me —what is the best way to catch them?"

"Oh," answered the fox, "you have only to go out upon the ice of the frozen lake, cut a hole in it, and stick your tail down into it. Then wait for the fish to bite. It may sting a little when they bite, but that should not matter, and the longer you sit there, the more fish you are likely to catch. When you think you have caught enough fish, just pull out your tail very quickly. It must be a good strong pull—be sure of that."

"I'll do it," said the bear, "and thank you very much for your advice."

Down to the frozen lake went the bear. He cut a hole in the ice. He put his tail through the hole —and waited.

It was very cold, and very soon the bear's tail began to hurt. "Aha!" he thought. "The fish are beginning to bite." And he kept his tail in place.

Later on, the bear tried to stand up, but he couldn't. The water in the lake had turned to ice and the bear was held fast by his tail.

Then he remembered what the fox had said— and he gave a very sharp, strong pull.

When the bear looked, he found no fish on the end of his tail. And he could hardly see his tail! Most of it was left frozen in the ice!

Ever since that day, all bears have had only stumpy tails.

The Gingerbread Boy

ONCE there was a little old woman and a little old man, and they lived together in a little old house. They didn't have any children at all, so one day the little old woman made a boy out of gingerbread. She planned to give him a chocolate jacket, with cinnamon seeds for buttons, and two fine, fat raisins for eyes.

When the little old woman had rolled him out, and pinched his gingerbread shoes into shape, she put him in a pan. Then she put the pan in the oven.

Some time later, she opened the oven door and pulled out the pan. Out jumped the little Gingerbread Boy. Out of the door and down the street he ran. The little old woman and the little old man ran after him, but he just laughed and shouted, "Run, run, as fast as you can! You can't catch me, I'm the Gingerbread Man!"

The little Gingerbread Boy ran on and on, until he came to a cow by the roadside. "Stop, little Gingerbread Boy," said the cow. "I want to eat you."

The little Gingerbread Boy laughed and said, "I've run away from a little old woman and a little old man, and I can run away from you, too, I can!"

And the cow couldn't catch him.

The little Gingerbread Boy ran on until he came to a horse in the pasture. "You look good to eat," said the horse, and he ran after him.

But the little Gingerbread Boy laughed and said, "I've run away from a little old woman, a little old man, and a cow, and I can run away from you, too, I can!"

And the horse couldn't catch him.

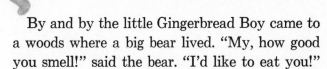

By and by the little Gingerbread Boy came to a woods where a big bear lived. "My, how good you smell!" said the bear. "I'd like to eat you!"

But the little Gingerbread Boy laughed and said, "I've run away from a little old woman, a little old man, a cow and a horse, and I can run away from you, too, I can!"

And the bear couldn't catch him.

By this time the little Gingerbread Boy was sure that nobody could catch him. He saw a fox coming across a field. The fox shouted at him and began to run. But the little Gingerbread Boy shouted across to him, "You can't catch me!"

The fox began to run faster, and the little Gingerbread Boy ran faster. As he ran, he said, "I've run away from a little old woman, a little old man, a cow, a horse, and a bear, and I can run away from you, too, I can! Run, run, as fast as you can! You can't catch me, I'm the Gingerbread Man!"

After swimming a little farther, the fox said, "You will get wet there. You had better jump on my shoulder."

So the little Gingerbread Boy jumped on his shoulder.

When they were near the other side of the river, the fox said, "My back is tired. You had better jump on my nose." So the little Gingerbread Boy jumped on his nose.

As soon as the fox reached the shore, he threw back his head. Into his mouth fell the little Gingerbread Boy, and the fox gobbled him up.

"Why," said the fox, "I would not catch you if I could. I would not even think of it."

Just then, the little Gingerbread Boy came to a river. But he could not swim.

"Jump on my tail and I will take you across," said the fox. So the Gingerbread Boy jumped on the fox's tail, and the fox swam into the river. A little distance from the shore he said, "Little Gingerbread Boy, I think you had better get on my back, or you may fall off."

So the little Gingerbread Boy jumped on his back.

And that was the end of the Gingerbread Boy.

The Milkmaid and Her Pail

A MILKMAID was on her way to market, carrying a pail of milk on the top of her head. As she walked along the road in the warm sunshine, she began to think of all the things she would buy with the money she was going to receive for the milk.

"I will buy some hens," she told herself, "and they will lay eggs every day. Then I will sell the eggs at the market, and with the money I will buy myself a new green dress with a green ribbon. Then I will go to the fair. All the young men will want to be my dancing partner, but I will toss my curls and say 'no' to every one of them."

As she spoke, the milkmaid tripped on a stone. Down came the pail of milk, spilling over the ground. Nothing was left but an empty pail and the scolding she knew she would receive when she returned home.

"That," she said to herself as she lay on the ground, "will teach me not to count my chickens before they are hatched!"

The Lion and the Mouse

ONE DAY a little mouse was scurrying through the jungle when she came upon what looked like a big pile of fur. She scampered upon it, and suddenly the pile of fur came to life. It was a great big lion! He had been sleeping, and the little mouse had wakened him.

"How dare you wake me up!" roared the lion. "Just for that I'm going to eat you up."

"No! No! Please don't!" begged the little mouse. "Let me go, Mr. Lion. You will not be sorry, for some day I may be able to do you a good turn."

"Ho, ho!" roared the lion, shaking with laughter. "How could a small creature like yourself do anything for me?" But he had a good heart, and he let the mouse go.

Soon afterwards, the lion was caught in a net. He roared and thrashed around, trying to free himself, but the ropes that bound him were too strong. The little mouse heard his cries, and came running to help him. With her sharp little teeth she gnawed at the ropes until they broke. And when the lion had stepped out of the net and was free once more, the little mouse said to him, "Now you can see why you should never laugh at those who are smaller than yourself."

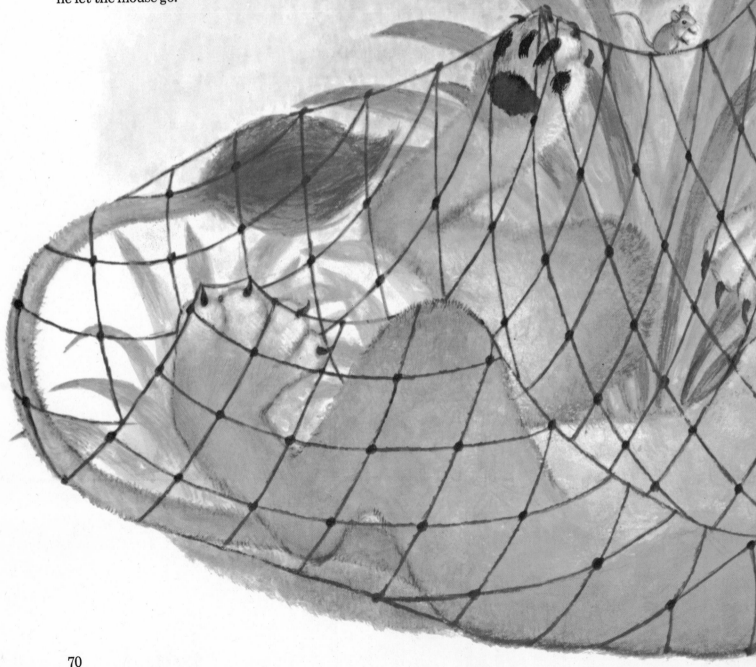

The Moon Maiden

At the foot of Mt. Fuji in far-off Japan, there once lived an honest, hard-working bamboo-cutter and his wife. They loved each other dearly, but they had no children, and so they were not happy.

"Ah, husband," mourned the wife, "more welcome to me than cherry blossoms in springtime would be a child of my own."

One evening the wife stood on her porch, looking up toward the snows that capped the mountain in beautiful white splendor, and she cried out to it:

"Fuji-san, I am sad because no childish laughter gladdens our home. Send me a little one to comfort me, I pray."

As she spoke, a glittering light suddenly shone forth from the summit of the mountain.

"Husband, come quickly," cried the woman. "See there on Fujiyama—the bright smiling face of a child!"

"I am sure it is only your imagination," replied the bamboo-cutter, "but I will climb the mountain and see what is there."

So he followed the trail of light through the forest and up the steep slope where Fujiyama towered above him. At last he stopped beneath a bamboo tree near a stream, from which the glow seemed to come. There, cradled in the branches, he found a tiny moon child.

"Ah, beautiful child, who are you?" he cried.

"I am the Princess Moonbeam," answered the child. "The Moon Lady is my mother, but she has sent me to comfort the sad heart of your wife."

"I will take you home where you will live as our child," the woodman said, and he carried her carefully down the mountain to his wife. "See what the Moon Lady has sent you," he said.

The wife was overjoyed. Her longing was satisfied at last.

As the years passed, Princess Moonbeam brought nothing but joy to the woodman and his wife. She was so lovely and so good that all who saw her loved her.

One day the Mikado himself came riding by. He saw how Princess Moonbeam brightened the humble cottage in which she lived, and he fell in love with her. He would have taken her back to his palace as his bride, for she was now grown up, but the wish of the earthly mother and father for a child had now been fulfilled, and the time had come for her to return to her sky mother, the Moon Lady.

"Stay with me on earth!" cried the Mikado.

"Stay with us on earth!" cried the bamboo-cutter and his wife.

Then the Mikado set two thousand archers on guard about the house, and even on the roof, so that no one might get through to claim the Moon Maiden. But it was no use. When the moon rose white and full, a silvery bridge of light arched down the sky to the earth, and along its path came the Moon Lady, while the Mikado's soldiers stood as though turned to stone. The Moon Lady passed straight through their ranks and bent down for her child, wrapping her in silver mist. Then she led her gently back to the sky.

As Princess Moonbeam traveled back to her home, she wept silvery tears for those she was leaving behind. And her bright shining tears took wings and floated away to carry a message of love that would comfort the Mikado and her earthly mother and father.

To this very day, the tears of Princess Moonbeam may be seen floating about the marshes and groves of Japan. The children run after them and say, "See the fireflies—how beautiful they are!"

Then their mothers, in the shadow of Fujiyama, tell the children this story—how the fireflies are glimmering love messages of the little Princess Moonbeam, fluttering down from her home in the sky.

The Wonderful Porridge Pot

ONCE there was a little girl who lived all alone with her mother. They were so poor that they often had nothing to eat.

As the little girl went out one morning to see what food she could find for herself and her mother, she met a very old woman. The old woman was carrying a porridge pot.

"Take this pot," said the old woman to the little girl, handing it over. "Say to it, 'Little pot, boil!' and it will magically boil sweet porridge for you. When you want it to stop, say, 'Little pot, stop!'"

Strange as this sounded, the child took the pot and returned home to her mother. She set the pot on the table and gave it the command: "Little pot, boil!"

Immediately, the pot set about boiling in the merriest way and the little girl and her mother had enough food for many, many days.

But one day, when the little girl had gone out of the house, the mother thought she would try out the wonderful porridge pot by herself. She set the pot on the table and gave the command: "Little pot, boil!"

The porridge pot obeyed. It boiled and bubbled, and bubbled and boiled, until it was full to the brim. Then the mother wished to have it stop boiling—but she could not remember what it was she was supposed to say!

The little porridge pot just kept right on boiling. It spilled over the kitchen table and onto the floor. Soon the whole kitchen was filled with porridge—and, yes, next the whole house was full. It came out of the windows and it came out of the doors. It poured out into the yard and then down the street. There was enough porridge to feed the whole town!

Still, no one was able to stop it!

At last, only one house in town was not full of porridge—and that was the house where the little girl had gone. When she looked out the window and saw the stream of porridge coming, she called out loudly, "Little pot, stop!"

It was none too soon. The pot stopped boiling, of course—but all the people had to EAT their way back to their houses again!

Puss in Boots

SOME YEARS ago a miller died, leaving three sons. He left his mill to the eldest son and his donkey to the second son. But he left only his cat to the youngest son. The youngest son did not know what good a cat was. But one day the cat said to him, "Master, give me a pair of boots and a bag, and you will see that I am not as useless as you think." So the miller's son gave the cat a pair of boots and a bag.

Puss in Boots went out into the forest. He caught some wild game and took it to the king. "Here is a present for you," he said, "from my master, the Marquis of Carabas." For a long time after that, Puss in Boots kept bringing presents to the king. Each time he told the king they were from his master, the Marquis of Carabas.

One day, the king decided to take his beautiful daughter for a ride in his carriage. Puss in Boots heard about it and ran home. He said, "Master, go quickly and wash in the river and I will make your fortune for you." So the miller's son went to the river.

When the king came riding by, Puss in Boots rushed up to the carriage. He cried out at the top of his voice, "Help! Help! Thieves have robbed my master, the Marquis of Carabas. They have thrown him into the river. He is drowning!"

The king remembered that the Marquis of Carabas had given him many fine presents and he wanted to help him. He told his men to pull the Marquis out of the river. Then the king told his men to bring fine clothes for the Marquis to wear. After the Marquis was dressed, he was invited to sit in the carriage beside the princess.

Meanwhile, Puss in Boots ran ahead. He came to some farmers, and said, "The king will soon ride by in his carriage. If he asks you who owns all this fine land, tell him it belongs to the Marquis of Carabas." The farmers agreed to do so. When the king heard this, he thought, "The Marquis of Carabas must be a very rich lord!"

Then Puss in Boots ran to a big castle that was owned by an ogre. He said to the ogre, "I have heard that you can change yourself into all kinds of animals. But I cannot believe it until I see you do it." The ogre changed himself into a fierce lion and roared. Then he changed himself back into an ogre and said, "You see!"

Puss in Boots said, "Yes, but a lion is a big animal. Can you also change yourself into a tiny mouse?" The ogre nodded, and changed himself into a tiny mouse. The minute the ogre became a mouse, Puss in Boots pounced on him and ate him up.

By this time the king's carriage was before the castle. The king thought, "The man who owns this castle must be a rich lord, indeed." At that moment, Puss in Boots came out of the castle. He took off his plumed hat and bowed low to the king. "Welcome, Your Majesty, to this castle of my master, the Marquis of Carabas," he said.

The king was now sure that the Marquis of Carabas was a very great lord, so he gave the princess in marriage to the Marquis and held a great wedding feast for them. The miller's son thus became a real lord.

As for Puss in Boots—he became a great lord, too, and lived happily in the palace.

The Morning Glory

ONCE, very long ago, a mother wren and her little baby wren lived in a nest high up near the top of a tree. The baby wren was so little that he could not yet fly, so he stayed in the nest the whole day through.

Each day Mother Wren would leave the nest to find food for herself and the little one, and when she returned she always told the baby wren about the beautiful things she saw. Especially did she mention the morning-glory, a lovely plant which at that time grew flat on the ground.

"Oh, how I wish that I could see the morning-glory!" the little wren told his mother.

Now the morning-glory heard this and it wanted to show itself to the little wren, but—what a pity!—it had not yet learned to climb. It pulled itself along the ground slowly, moving toward the foot of the tree.

Finally, as it wanted to go up so much, the morning-glory caught hold of the bark of the tree. Then, not knowing quite how, but doing it all the same, it pulled itself up a little. Up, up, up it went—more surely with each try—and soon it reached the edge of the nest, where the little wren could see it.

Morning-glories have climbed ever since.

The Elves and the Shoemaker

ONCE there was a kind old shoemaker who had grown very poor. In fact, he had only enough leather left to make one pair of shoes.

"Look, wife," he said. "I'll cut these out this evening before we go to bed. Then in the morning I can finish them."

After that, he said his prayers and went to bed. In the morning, he went to his workbench, and what do you think? Instead of two pieces of leather, there stood a neat pair of shoes.

"Wife! Wife!" he called in amazement, and she came running. Together they looked at the shoes and found them beautifully stitched, but neither the shoemaker nor his wife could imagine who could have made them.

Soon a customer came in.

"What fine shoes!" he exclaimed, and offered much money for them—so much that the shoemaker was able to buy leather for two more pairs and still have some money left over to buy bread and milk.

That evening he cut out two pairs of shoes from the leather he had bought, and went to bed feeling happy. The next morning he sang as he walked toward his workbench. Then once again he stopped in astonishment, for there stood two more neat pairs of shoes, sewn with the greatest of care.

"So well made!" said the customers who came to the shop. "See the fine stitches! See how beautifully they are shaped!"

The shoemaker quickly sold those two pairs and found that he had money to buy leather for four more pairs.

And so it went. Each night, before he went to

bed, he would cut out the leather; and every morning, when he got up, he would find it all made up into the neatest shoes imaginable. Soon the shoemaker and his wife were not poor at all.

One evening just before Christmas, the shoemaker said to his wife, "Let's stay up all night and see who has been helping us so kindly."

"That's a fine idea," said the shoemaker's wife.

So they hid in a corner and settled down to wait. On the stroke of midnight, in came two little elves who hopped up onto the workbench and set busily to work. Their fingers flew so fast, stitching and sewing, hammering and tapping, that the shoemaker could not take his eyes off them. In no time at all there were finished shoes on the bench. Then the little men skipped lightly out of the room.

"The elves have made us rich," said the shoemaker's wife next morning, "and yet the poor little things haven't any clothes to wear. Wouldn't it be nice if we could do something for them to show them how grateful we are?"

"Oh, yes!" said the shoemaker. "I'll make them some tiny shoes, and you do the rest."

"Coat and hat and trousers," said his wife. "Shirt and vest and stockings—all about the size of doll clothes!"

And she and her husband went happily to work. Two days before Christmas, everything was finished. That evening, the shoemaker and his wife left no leather on the workbench. Instead, they spread out the pretty little clothes, and hid themselves in the corner.

At midnight, the elves came skipping in. When they saw the presents laid out for them, their eyes almost popped out of their heads. Quickly they slipped into their new clothes and skipped around the room singing,

"Tonight we have no time to sew—
We'll wear these clothes and off we'll go!"

And with that, they went out the door, still singing. The shoemaker and his wife never saw them again; but their good luck remained, and they lived happily to the end of their days.

The Little Girl and the Hare

Once a woman had a pretty green garden with cabbages in it. But a little hare came each day and ate the cabbages. Then the woman said to her little girl, "Go into the garden and chase the hare away."

So the little girl said to the hare, "Shoo, shoo, little hare! You are eating up all our cabbages."

Said the hare, "Little girl, come, sit on my tail and go with me to my house."

But the little girl would not go. The next day the hare came again and ate the cabbages. And the mother said again, "Go into the garden and chase the hare away."

So the little girl said to the hare, "Shoo, shoo, little hare! You are eating up all our cabbages."

Said the hare, "Little girl, come, sit on my tail and go with me to my house."

But the little girl would not go. The third day the hare came again. By this time the little girl had grown very curious to see the little hare's house. So when he invited her to go with him, she seated herself on his tail and off they went.

84

The little hare took her through the woods to his little house. And a nice house it was. But when the hare got the little girl inside, he rose upon his hind legs and shouted:

"You shall stay here forever and be my cook! Put those cabbages in the kettle. Cook them. I shall ask some friends to come and have dinner with me."

Then he went away, locking the door behind him.

Now the little girl was sad. She didn't want to stay with the hare forever, she wanted to go

And there they were outside the house — a hare, a crow, and a fox. Away went the hare to keep them outside until all was ready in the house. And he locked the door behind him. But the little girl stopped crying and sprang up. She got some straw from the hare's bed, made it into a doll, put her own dress and apron on it and set it up near the stove. Then she ran to the place where the door would hide her when the hare unlocked it and swung it open.

In he came. He thought the doll by the kettle was the little girl and he shouted, "Take off the lid! Serve supper! My guests are hungry!" But the doll didn't move. So he ran and slapped it hard. Over it fell. Then he saw it was just a straw doll. In a rage, he looked about for the little girl, but she was already out the door and on her way home to her mother.

home to her mother. But she put the cabbages on the stove to cook. Presently, the hare came back and shouted:

"Set the table! Set the table! My guests are coming!" Then he went away again, locking the door behind him.

But the little girl didn't set the table. She sat down on a stool and cried. Pretty soon the hare came back. He was furious when he saw the table wasn't set, and he shouted:

"Set the table! Set the table! My guests are HERE!"

The Three Wishes

Once, many years ago, there was a poor wood-cutter and his wife who lived from day to day in a humble cottage near the edge of the woods. Every day the man would go into the forest to chop wood and return in time for supper. Then the couple talked about the good things that their neighbors owned, and wished that they, too, might have such good things.

One day, while the woodcutter was in the forest, he said aloud, as he had often said before, "Oh, it is a hard life! I have to work so hard all day long, and yet I am still poor. There are so many things I would like to have—if only I could ever hope to get them!"

As he uttered these words, a beautiful fairy appeared before him. "I have heard your complaints," she said, "and so, I shall grant you three wishes. Choose them wisely, because you may have no more than three." Then she faded from view as mysteriously as she had appeared.

When the woodcutter went home that evening, he told his wife what had happened, and they were both so excited they could hardly eat. "Imagine!" said the wife. "We can ask for anything we like—anything! Oh, I'm so happy!"

"Yes, it is wonderful," agreed the man. "Just think—we can have great wealth!"

"Or a fine house," said his wife.

"Even a mansion—or a palace," added the husband, his eyes shining brightly.

They went on talking in this way, thinking of all the things they could possibly wish for, but they could not agree on any one wish right away, so they decided to put it off until the next day. Then they sat down to the table to eat.

The man looked at the bowl of soup that was before him and sighed. "Oh, dear, soup again!" he said. "How I wish for once that I could have a nice fat sausage!"

Wonder of wonders, at that very instant, a plump sausage appeared magically on the table!

The wife was the first to realize what had happened. "Now see what you have done!" she cried. "You have wasted a wish on a silly old sausage. Now we have only two wishes left!"

"Oh, well, there is still much to be wished for," said the man.

"Is that all you have to say for yourself?" scolded the woman. "Here you have wasted a perfectly good wish for all time. How could you have been so foolish?" And she went on like that, complaining loudly.

Soon the man lost his patience and exclaimed, "I am tired of hearing about the sausage! I am tired of hearing you speak! I wish that the sausage were stuck to your nose!"

No sooner were the words out of his mouth than the sausage was hanging at the end of his wife's nose!

"Now see what you have done!" cried the wife. "You have wasted another wish by your foolish tongue!" And she tried desperately to remove the sausage from the end of her nose, but it would not come off.

"We still have one wish left," said the husband. "We can still wish for great wealth."

"What good is money or riches," the woman asked, "if I must go through life with a sausage on the end of my nose? Everyone would laugh at me and I could not abide that! No, there is only one thing to do, and that is to wish it off."

"But then we will be left as poor as we were before," said the husband.

"That is all that I wish for," said the wife. And in a flash, the sausage was gone.

The three wishes had been granted, and for all of their plans, the woodcutter and his wife were no better off. In fact, sad to say, they could not even have sausage for dinner.

Rose Red

ONCE there was a poor widow who had a daughter as beautiful as the roses that grew in the garden. She was therefore named Rose Red.

One cold winter night a knock came at the door. "See who is there," said the woman. "It may be some traveler who has lost his way."

Rose Red raised the latch, but upon seeing a bear outside she became frightened and started to bolt the door again.

"Do not be afraid, I will do you no harm!" the bear cried. "I am half frozen and only want to warm myself."

"You poor bear," said the girl sweetly. "Come in and sit by the fire." And she took a broom and brushed the snow from his fur.

"I shall not forget your kindness," the bear replied.

Indeed, he was so friendly and such good company that both mother and daughter were glad to have him. They looked forward to his coming each night, and left the door unbolted until he arrived.

When spring came and everything was green again, the bear said one morning to Rose Red, "Now I must go away, and may not come again the whole summer."

"Where are you going, dear Bear?" she asked.

"I must go into the wood and guard my treasure from the bad dwarfs," he replied.

Rose Red was very sorry that her friend had to leave. She opened the door, but as the bear ran out, a piece of his fur caught on the latch. It seemed to her that she saw gold shining through, but she was not certain.

One day as she was walking through the woods, she came upon a dwarf.

"What are you staring at?" he cried angrily. "Help me out of this!"

"What is the matter?" she asked.

"You silly girl, can't you see I am caught in this tree?"

The dwarf had driven a wedge in the tree to split it, but somehow had caught his beard in the crack. When the wood closed over it, he found he was stuck fast.

Rose Red tugged and tugged, but she could not get the ugly little man free. At last she, was forced to take out her scissors and cut off his beard.

As soon as the dwarf was free he seized a sack of gold lying at the roots of the tree. "You nasty girl, cutting off my beautiful beard," he growled.

"May evil reward you!" And he stalked off.

Several weeks later Rose Red was walking in the woods again and she heard someone screaming. It was the same dwarf. This time a huge eagle had seized him in his claws and was about to fly off with him. Quickly Rose Red ran to him and pulled with all her might, and after a struggle the eagle let go and flew away.

When the dwarf recovered from his fright he said in a shrill voice, "Could you not deal more gently with me? You have torn my clothes!" Then he picked up a sack of jewels and disappeared.

Rose Red continued on her way, but later in the day she saw the dwarf again. He was busy counting the jewels from the sack, and had them piled up on the ground. How they glittered in the light from the setting sun!

When he saw the maiden his face grew red with anger. "Why are you spying on me?" he cried. "Begone, or I shall strike you dead!"

At these words there was a great roaring and a black bear rushed out of the woods toward them. The dwarf tried to get away, but he was too late; the bear was already upon him.

"Dear Mr. Bear," he said, trembling, "spare me and you shall have all my treasure. Give me my life! What do you want with a poor little thin dwarf? Eat the girl instead—she will be a much tenderer morsel for you. Pray let me go!"

The bear did not answer, but gave the evil dwarf a blow with his paw, and he fell over dead.

Rose Red started to run away. "Do not be frightened," the bear said, and Rose Red recognized the voice of her old friend!

As he walked toward her, his skin suddenly fell off; and, behold, he was not a bear, but a handsome young man dressed all in gold!

"I am a king's son," he said. "I was changed by the wicked dwarf into a wild bear. When you were so kind to me, even though I was a bear, the dwarf lost his evil powers. Now that he is dead, the spell is broken, and I am freed!"

How happy Rose Red was that her friend, the bear, was really a handsome prince! They went home together and told her mother all that had happened. The prince declared his love for the maiden and asked her mother's blessing. This the poor widow gladly gave, and Rose Red and the king's son were married that very day.

The Farmer, His Son, and Their Donkey

ONE day, a farmer and his son were on their way to market. With them was their donkey, who carried their vegetables and fruit in baskets on his back. The day was very warm, and as they walked along the road, the man on one side of the donkey and the boy on the other, they had to stop often and wipe their brows.

Presently, they passed a farmer's wife standing in her doorway.

The farmer tipped his hat and said cordially, "Good morning. It's a nice day, isn't it?"

"Good morning, indeed!" replied the woman. "It's a hot morning, that's what it is, and bound to get hotter, and there you are, making that poor child walk in the sun. If he faints from the heat, it will be all your fault!"

The man stopped and thought about this. "She is right," he said at last, and he moved the baskets to make room for his son on the donkey's back.

The boy was not comfortable on the crowded donkey and he really liked to walk, but he said nothing.

They went on a little farther until they passed a group of country people. An old man in the group cried out, "What a good-for-nothing boy! You ride while your poor old father walks. Shame on you!"

The farmer stopped and thought for a bit. Then he asked his son to climb down from the donkey.

"Let your poor old father ride," he said.

His father was neither poor nor old and the boy knew it, but he climbed down and let his father take his place.

Then they started off again. As they neared the edge of the town, they met a man riding a horse.

"Why aren't you both riding the donkey?" the man asked. "It's silly not to. I really think the donkey is smarter than the two of you!"

And he rode on, shaking his head at such a show of stupidity.

"He's right," said the farmer. "It is silly for one of us to walk when we both can ride!"

It wasn't easy to make room on the donkey for both of them, but somehow they did so. Then they went on, more slowly now, until they reached the town. Presently they met a group of townspeople standing and talking together.

"Just look at that!" cried a woman. "How cruel to make that poor little donkey carry such a heavy load!"

"Yes, you should be ashamed!" said one of the men. "You and your son are strong enough to carry the donkey. What clods you are!"

The farmer stopped and scratched his head. At last he said, "My son, they are right. We must always be kind to dumb animals. We will carry our donkey the rest of the way."

So they lifted down the baskets of vegetables and fruit, and the farmer cut a pole and tied the donkey's legs to it. Then he put one of the baskets over his son's shoulders. The rest he carried himself.

And so they went on, carrying the donkey upside down between them.

In a little while, they came to a bridge and started across. A group of boys were coming the other way. They took one look at the donkey on the pole and burst out laughing, pointing and making fun of the farmer and his son. They made so much noise that soon a large crowd gathered to join in the laughter.

All this noise frightened the donkey, who hated being carried upside down anyway, and he began to struggle and kick. The ropes binding him to the pole broke, and father, son, produce, and donkey all fell *ker-splash!* into the water. The farmer and his son swam safely to shore, but by then the donkey had run away, and all the vegetables and fruit were at the bottom of the stream.

The farmer shook his head. "My son," he said, "always remember one thing: when you try to please everyone, you end up by pleasing no one."

The Mice and the Cat

A CERTAIN cat who lived in a great country house was so quick and so watchful that the mice found themselves in danger every minute. So one night the eldest of the mice called a meeting to discuss the matter.

One by one, the mice stood up and told about their narrow escapes from the cat, and then each suggested a plan that would end their fears and let them live in peace. But none of the plans seemed good enough.

Then a young mouse stood up. He said he had a plan that could not fail to win the approval of all.

"If," said he, "the cat wore a bell around her neck, every step she took would make it tinkle. Then we would know when she was coming and would have time to run home. By this simple means, we could all live in safety."

A murmur of approval arose from the gathering. The young mouse sat down, very pleased with himself. Then an old gray mouse, with a merry twinkle in his eyes, stood up and faced his friends.

"It is a good plan, as far as it goes," he agreed. "But," he asked, "who will be the one to put the bell around the cat's neck?"

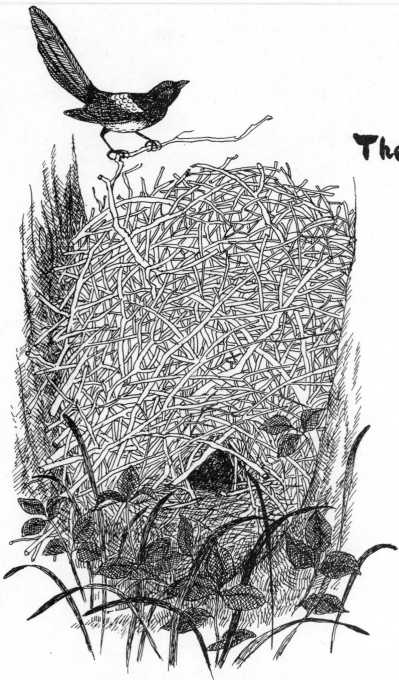

The Magpie's Nest

"I shall be glad to show you how," said the magpie. "But you must watch everything I do. First, I lay two sticks across each other, so."

"To be sure," said the crow. "I knew it must begin with two sticks. They should be crossed, of course."

"Then mix some straw and some moss in this way," said the magpie.

"Oh, yes, certainly," said the jackdaw. "I guessed all that without being taught."

"Then more moss, more straw and feathers, like this," continued the magpie.

"Yes, yes," said the sparrow. "I knew that was the way to do it."

Still the magpie went on, but the birds acted as if they knew everything he told them. At last he would tell them no more, though the nest was built up only halfway.

"If you knew all about nest-building," he said, "why did you come here to learn it from me? Go and build your own nests. I'll not tell you how I built mine."

Then away they all flew. And each bird set to work to build himself a nest. But when they had built up halfway, they stopped, for they did not know how to go on.

So to this day their nests all look like the magpie's, just cut in two.

Long, long ago, when the world was young, the birds did not know how to build nests for themselves.

The only bird that knew how to build a nest well was the magpie. His nest was covered all over, except for a hole where he went in and out.

The other birds talked a great deal about the wonderful little house which the magpie could build, and they wished they might build one just like it. So one day two birds of every kind went to see the magpie. "We have come to learn how to build nests for ourselves and our little birds. We will pay you well if you will show us how," they said.

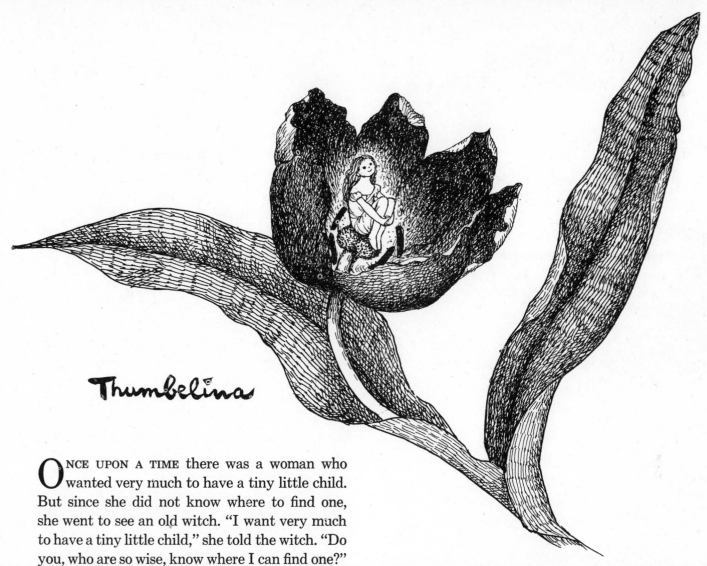

Thumbelina

ONCE UPON A TIME there was a woman who wanted very much to have a tiny little child. But since she did not know where to find one, she went to see an old witch. "I want very much to have a tiny little child," she told the witch. "Do you, who are so wise, know where I can find one?"

"Indeed I do," replied the witch. "Here is a barleycorn for you. It may look like an ordinary grain of barley, such as farmers grow in their fields, but it is not. Plant it in a flowerpot the moment you get home, and you shall see what you shall see."

"Thank you," said the woman, and she gave the witch twelve pennies to pay for the barleycorn. Then she hurried home and planted it, as the witch had told her to do. In a short while, a fine big flower came up. It looked very much like a tulip, but the petals were tightly closed, as though it were still a bud.

"What a beautiful flower!" said the woman, and she kissed it on its folded petals. At this, the flower opened with a loud POP! It was indeed a tulip, and in the center, on the green cushion of the flower, sat a tiny girl. She was as pretty as she could be, but she was no bigger than your thumb.

The woman was delighted. "I shall call you Thumbelina," she said.

At night, Thumbelina slept in a polished walnut shell, on a mattress made of blue violet petals. A rose petal was her coverlet. In the daytime, she played on a table on which the woman had placed a plate filled with water, surrounded by many flowers. Thumbelina amused herself by floating across the plate of water on a tulip leaf, rowing with two oars made of horsehair. It was a joy to watch her, and to hear her sing in a voice as clear as a tiny silver bell. Surely such singing had never been heard before!

One night, as she lay in her pretty little bed, a big ugly old toad hopped in through a broken pane in the window, and jumped right on the table where Thumbelina lay sleeping. "What a lovely creature!" said the old toad to herself. "She will make a charming wife for my son." And with that she picked up the walnut shell with Thumbelina in it and leaped through the window again, back into the garden.

A broad stream flowed through the garden, and in its marshy banks the old toad lived with her son. Ugh! He was even uglier than his mother. When he saw the pretty little girl in her lovely bed, all he could say was, "Koax, koax, brek-ek-ek!"

"Sssh!" said his mother. "Don't talk so loud!

You'll wake her and she'll fly away, for she's as light as thistledown. We'll put her on that big water lily leaf in the middle of the stream, so she can't get away, while we prepare our best room under the marsh for you to live in after you're married."

Many water lilies grew in the stream, their broad leaves floating in the water. The largest of these leaves was much farther from the shore than any of the others, and on this leaf the old toad placed the walnut shell with the sleeping girl in it.

When Thumbelina woke up the next morning and saw where she was, she began to weep bitterly, for there was water all around the leaf and no way to reach the shore. Meanwhile, the old mother toad was working hard down in the mud, getting their home ready to receive her new daughter-in-law. At last she swam out to the leaf with her horrible son. They came to take Thumbelina's pretty little bed down into the bridal chamber before the bride herself was conducted into it. The old toad bowed low in the water and said, "This is my dear son. He is to be your dear husband, and you will live happily together down in the thick mud!"

"Koax, koax, brek-ek-ek!" was all her son could say.

Then they took the little bed and swam away with it, leaving Thumbelina weeping on the green leaf, for the thought of living in the mud with the old toad and her son was more than she could

bear. The little fishes swimming in the water under the leaf had heard everything. Now they lifted their heads out of the water to see the little girl. "What a darling she is!" they said, and were much distressed at the thought of her living down in the mud with the hideous toad. No, no, such a thing must never be!

So all the fishes surrounded the green stalk of the water lily leaf, and gnawed it with their teeth until the leaf was separated from the stalk and floated away down the stream, carrying Thumbelina with it, far away from the toad and her son.

Past many towns sailed Thumbelina, and the birds in the trees saw her and sang, "What a sweet little girl!" On and on floated the leaf, until at last it came to another land. Thumbelina laughed and sang as she floated along, for now there was nothing to fear, and the land through which she sailed was very beautiful. The sun, shining on the water, turned it to liquid gold, and the air was filled with the fragrance of many flowers.

At last the leaf floated too close to the shore and became caught among some of the stones jutting out into the water. But Thumbelina was able to leap safely to the shore.

All summer long, Thumbelina lived alone in the forest. She wove a bed for herself out of some blades of grass, and she hung the little bed under a great burdock leaf so that she could be sheltered from the rain. She dined on honey which she sucked from the flowers, and she drank the dew each morning from the leaves.

In this way the summer and fall went by; and then came the long, cold winter. All the birds who had sung so sweetly for her had flown away. The trees lost their leaves and the flowers withered. The burdock leaf under which she had lived shriveled up until nothing was left of it but a withered stalk.

Thumbelina was terribly cold, for her clothes had been worn threadbare and she was a delicate little thing. She would surely freeze to death! Snow began to fall, and every time a snowflake struck her it was as if she had been hit by a whole shovelful, since she was scarcely larger than a snowflake herself! Poor Thumbelina wandered around, seeking a warm place to spend the winter.

Near the edge of the wood where she had now arrived stood a large cornfield, but the corn had been cut months ago, and nothing remained but hard stubble sticking up from the frozen ground. It was like struggling through a vast forest to Thumbelina, but she fought her way through it. Then she came to the door of a field mouse, who had a little hole under the stubble. It was a warm, cozy house and the mouse was happy, for she had a roomful of corn, as well as a kitchen and fine dining room. Thumbelina knocked on the door and when the field mouse opened it she begged for a bit of barley, because she hadn't had anything to eat for two days.

"You poor little thing!" said the field mouse, who was really a kind-hearted old creature. "Come in and have dinner with me." She took such a liking to Thumbelina that she said, "If you like, you may stay here all winter. Of course, I shall expect you to keep my rooms clean and tell me stories. I'm very fond of stories." Thumbelina did as the field mouse asked and in return she was well-treated and made comfortable.

One day, the field mouse said to her, "We shall have a visitor soon. He's my neighbor, who visits me every week. He is very rich, his rooms are very grand, and he wears a beautiful black velvet coat. What a good husband he would make for you! He can't see anything, so you must tell him some of your best stories."

But Thumbelina knew this neighbor was a mole, and she did not care to please him, much less marry him. He came to visit, dressed in his black velvet coat. He asked Thumbelina to sing for him and she did so. She sang, "Ladybug, Ladybug, fly away home," and other pretty songs, and the mole fell in love with her then and there, he was so charmed by her lovely voice. But, being a cautious fellow, he said nothing.

He had just dug a long tunnel through the ground from his house to that of the field mouse, and he now gave them permission to use it whenever they pleased. "There is a dead bird in the passage," he warned, "but don't let that frighten you."

The mole took a torch of decayed wood in his mouth and it shone like fire in the darkness, lighting the way for them. He led his friends through the tunnel, and when they came to the spot where the dead bird lay, the mole pushed a hole through the ceiling with his broad nose so the daylight could shine through.

It shone on the body of a swallow. His pretty wings were folded, and his head and claws were almost hidden under his feathers. Poor dear thing! thought Thumbelina. He must certainly have died of the cold. She waited until the others had turned away, and then she smoothed the feathers on the bird's head and kissed the closed eyelids. "Perhaps it was you who sang so sweetly to me in the summertime, darling bird," she whispered.

The mole closed up the hole that let in the daylight, and then he took the ladies home. That night Thumbelina could not sleep for thinking of the poor swallow, so she got up and wove a warm rug out of some soft hay. She took it to the dead bird and spread it over him, and tucked him in with some soft thistledown that she had found in the field mouse's room, so that he could lie warm in the cold earth.

"Good-by, dear pretty bird," she said. "Thank you for all your songs last summer, when the trees were green and the sun shone so brightly!"

As she said this, Thumbelina pressed her head against the dead bird's breast. Then she gave a cry of surprise. She had heard a faint beating inside the bird. It was the swallow's heart! He was not dead — only numbed from the cold. Thumbelina was overjoyed. She covered the bird more closely with the down, and ran and brought her own coverlet, a balsam leaf, to spread over his head.

The following night she tiptoed out to him again. He was alive and able to move, but still

very weak. He opened his eyes for a moment to look at Thumbelina, who stood with her lantern — a piece of torchwood — in her hand.

"Thank you, dear child," whispered the swallow. "I feel much better now, and soon I shall be strong enough to fly out into the warm sunshine."

"Oh, no!" cried Thumbelina. "You must not go outside now. It is winter and very cold. You must stay here in your warm bed and let me take care of you."

She brought the bird some water in a flower petal. The swallow drank it gratefully, and then told her how he had hurt his wing on a thorn bush and so could not fly as fast as his brothers. They had flown on, far, far away to the warm countries, while he had fallen unconscious to the ground. That was all he remembered, and he had no idea how he came to be there in the passage.

The swallow stayed in his warm bed all winter. Thumbelina cared for him tenderly, and when spring came the swallow was well and strong again. Thumbelina opened the hole in the ceiling made by the mole, and the warm sunshine poured into the tunnel. The swallow begged the little girl to fly away with him into the green wood. "You can sit on my back," he said. But Thumbelina shook her head. She knew how vexed the field mouse would be if she left like that. "No, I cannot go with you," she said. "I really cannot."

"Good-by, then, you pretty darling," said the swallow, and away he flew into the sunlight. Thumbelina watched him go, and tears streamed from her eyes, for she loved the swallow very much.

Now Thumbelina was truly sad. She was not allowed to go out into the sunshine. Moreover, the grain that was sown in the field above the field mouse's house grew so tall that it was like a dense forest.

"Well, now!" said the field mouse to Thumbelina one day soon after this. "You must start to work on your wedding clothes. Mr. Mole has asked for your hand in marriage, you lucky girl!"

She set Thumbelina to work turning the spindle, and she hired four spiders to weave day and night. Every evening, the mole came to call, and he always spoke of the time when summer would be over. Then they would be married. Just now, the sun shone so hotly that it burned the ground and made it hard as stone.

Thumbelina disliked the mole and did not listen to his tiresome conversation. She wished that she might see the dear swallow again, but he had doubtless flown far away, for he never came back.

Then it was autumn and Thumbelina's wedding day was at hand. All was in readiness. The mole came to fetch his bride and take her with him to his home underground. The little girl could not bear to think that she would never see the bright sun again. She ran to the door to have a last look at it.

"Good-by, dear sun," she said. Then she ventured a little way from the door, and threw her arms around a red flower growing close by. "Give my love to the swallow, if you ever see him!" she cried.

"Tweet-tweet-tweet!" She suddenly heard a twittering above her head. She looked up and there was the swallow flying past! He saw Thumbelina and flew down to her, overjoyed at seeing his dear friend again. Then Thumbelina told the bird everything that had happened since he left, and how she hated to marry the mole and live underground. As she talked, Thumbelina could not hold back the tears.

"Winter is coming soon," the swallow said, "and I am flying far away to the warm countries. Come with me! You can sit on my back. Tie yourself on with your sash, and we will fly far away from the ugly mole and his dark house. Please come with me, dear little Thumbelina! You saved my life when I lay frozen in the tunnel. Let me help you now."

"Yes, I will come with you!" said Thumbelina. She sat on the bird's back with her feet resting on his outspread wings, and tied her sash to his strongest feathers. Then the swallow rose up into the air and flew high over forest and lake, far away over the snow-capped mountains.

At length they came to the warm countries. How bright the sun shone, and how high the sky seemed! Thumbelina could only stare around her with wonder and delight. By the wayside were hedges on which grew marvelous green and blue grapes. Lemons and oranges hung from the trees. The air was fragrant with the scent of myrtle and thyme, and along the country lanes happy children were chasing brightly colored butterflies.

The swallow flew on, until at last they came to a lovely blue lake. By its side stood a white marble castle, shaded by tall trees.

"This is my home," said the swallow. "But I think you will be happier living among the flowers, rather than in a tree."

"That would be lovely," said Thumbelina. So the swallow flew down with her to the ground, and placed her on the petal of a large white flower, one of many blooming all around the castle.

But how surprised Thumbelina was to see, in the center of the flower, a little man, as shining and transparent as if he had been made of glass! On his head was a tiny golden crown, and he wore a pair of shining wings on his shoulders. He was scarcely taller than Thumbelina. He was the spirit of the flower. Such a tiny man or maid lived in every flower, but he was the king of them all.

"Oh, how beautiful he is!" Thumbelina whispered to the swallow.

The Flower King was startled to see the swallow, who seemed a giant of a bird to one so tiny, but when he saw Thumbelina, he was charmed. He thought her the prettiest girl he had ever seen, so he took his crown and placed it on her head.

Then he asked if he might know her name, and begged her to marry him and be Queen of all the flowers.

Here was a different kind of husband from the toad's son or the mole with his black velvet coat! Thumbelina replied, "Yes," at once.

At this, all the other flowers opened and out of them came little ladies and gentlemen. They all gave Thumbelina a present. But the best present of all was a pair of transparent wings which they fastened to Thumbelina's shoulders so that she could fly from flower to flower.

The swallow watched from a nest far above and sang his sweetest song, though he was sad at heart to be parted from the little girl, whom he loved so much.

"Good-by, good-by," sang the swallow, flying away to a home in faraway Denmark. There he had a nest outside the window of a man who could tell fairy tales. For him the swallow sang many sweet songs, and that is how we came to know this story.

Lazy Jack

LONG AGO, there was a boy named Jack who lived with his mother in a little house in the woods. They were very poor. Jack's mother begged her son to try to find work, but he would do nothing. At last she told him that unless he worked, he would have to go out into the world and make his own living.

So Jack decided that it would be wise to get some work to do. He looked about, and one fine morning he hired himself to a farmer. At the end of his day's work, the farmer gave him a penny. The lad put it into his handkerchief, but lost it on the way home.

"Silly!" cried his mother. "Why did you not put the penny into your pocket?"

"I shall be sure to do so next time," said Jack.

The next morning, he hired himself to a man who kept cows. When his work was finished, Jack received a jug of milk. Remembering his mother's words, he put the milk into his pocket, but before he reached home, it had spilled.

"You silly boy!" exclaimed his mother. "You should have carried the jug on your head."

"That I will do the next time," said Jack.

On the following day he hired himself to another farmer. For this day's work, he received a dozen eggs. Setting them on his head, he started off. But by the time he reached home, the eggs had all fallen off.

"Jack! Jack!" cried his mother. "You should have carried them in your hands."

"That I will do the next time," said Jack.

The following day he hired himself to a baker, who gave him a pig for his day's work.

Jack remembered what his mother had told him and he carried the pig in his hands. But it struggled so much that he had to let it go.

"Silly!" said his mother. "You should have tied a rope around its neck and pulled it home."

"I shall do so next time," promised Jack.

The next day he hired himself to a butcher who paid him with a side of bacon. Jack tied a rope to it, and pulled it along the road. But the dogs ran after it, and by the time he reached home they had eaten every bit of it.

"Jack," said his mother, "you should have carried it on your shoulder."

"Next time I shall do so," said Jack.

Once more he went off, and this time hired himself to a herdsman, who gave him a goat in payment. Remembering his mother's words, Jack pulled the goat up on his shoulder, and started off.

On the way he passed the house of a rich merchant who had an only child, a beautiful girl who had never laughed in her life. Her father had said that the man who could make her laugh could marry her.

As Jack passed by, with the goat across his shoulder, its legs sticking up in the air, the young girl happened to be looking out of her window. Jack and his strange burden made such a funny picture that she began to laugh.

Her father was overjoyed to think that at last his daughter was able to laugh, and without delay he gave Jack her hand in marriage.

On their wedding day Jack received a large sum of money from his bride's father. He bought a fine house, and he and his bride and his mother lived happily together for many, many years.

The Little House

ONCE upon a time, a jar rolled off a peasant's cart, and was left lying in the middle of a field. And a little mouse came running along and saw the jar lying there, and thought what a nice house it would make, and began to wonder who left it there.

And the little mouse said: "Little house, little house, who lives in the little house?"

And nobody answered. Then the little mouse looked in, and found no one there!

"Well, then," he said, "I shall live here myself." So he settled himself in the jar.

Then a frog came hopping along, and said: "Little house, little house, who lives in the little house?"

"I, Mr. Mouse, I live in the little house—and what sort of animal are you?" replied the mouse.

"I am Mr. Frog," replied the frog.

"Come in, then, and let's live together," said the mouse.

"Very well," replied the frog, and he hopped into the jar, and they began to live together.

Then a hare came running across the field. "Little house, little house, who lives in the little house?" he asked.

"Mr. Frog and Mr. Mouse, and who are you?"

"I am Mr. Hare who runs over the hills. May I come in, too?"

"Come in and live with us," they told him. "There's plenty of room."

Then a fox came running past, and said, "Little house, little house, who lives in the little house?"

"Mr. Hare, Mr. Frog, and Mr. Mouse," came the answer. "And what is YOUR name?"

"They call me Mr. Fox."

"Very well," they all said, "come in and live with us."

"Right you are!" said the fox, and he got into the jar, too. And all four began to live together. And they went on living there, until one day a bear came along out of the forest, and said, "Little house, little house, who lives in the little house?"

"Mr. Fox, Mr. Hare, Mr. Frog, and Mr. Mouse. And who are you?" they all answered.

"I am Mr. Bear Squash-you-all-flat!" replied the bear. And the bear sat down on the jar and squashed it flat.

The Foolish Weathercock

ONCE a weathercock stood on a tall steeple, in a little town by the sea. Sometimes the weathercock looked toward the sea. He could watch the white waves rolling in. He could watch the ships sailing. He could see the sea birds flying, and the children playing in the sand.

Sometimes he looked toward the land. Then he could watch the farmers cutting the hay and the grain. He could see them taking the sheep and the cows to pasture.

When the wind blew, the weathercock turned round and round. Every day, the sailors would look at the weathercock. If he turned to the east, they would say, "We must stay at home today." If he turned to the west, they would sing, "The weathercock says the wind's in the west, and the weathercock knows which wind is best." Then they would put out to sea.

Sometimes he told them that the wind would bring rain. Sometimes he stood still on his steeple, then turned around to the west, so the farmers knew that the day would be fair. Then they would go into the fields to work.

One day, the weathercock began to think how important he was. At first this pleased him, and he sang, "Oh, farmers and sailors must look at me, before tilling the ground or sailing the sea."

Then he began to wonder if the farmers and the sailors knew how important he was.

"They never thank me," he said. "Why do I work for them? I will stop!"

Then a wind came by. It said to the grain, "Bow down!" And the grain in the wide fields bowed down before the wind. It said to the trees, "Bow down!" And all the trees bowed before the wind.

Then it said to the weathercock, "Turn! Turn!" But the weathercock would not turn. So the wind blew the weathercock right off the top of the steeple, and it lay on the ground all night.

"Now," said the little weathercock, "the farmers and the sailors will know how important I am! They will miss me in the morning. How sorry they will be!"

In the morning, the sailors looked to see the weathercock on the steeple. He was not there. But they saw the smoke trailing up from the chimneys. So they sang, "The smoke clouds say that the wind's from the west, and the smoke clouds know which wind is best." And they put out to sea.

The farmers, too, looked for the little weathercock, but he was not on the steeple. They saw the leaves on the trees turning to the west, and so they went to work in the fields.

Now the little weathercock was sad as it lay on the ground. "The sailors and the farmers did not need me," he said. "Why didn't I turn with the wind?"

In the afternoon, some men came. They put the weathercock back in his place on top of the steeple.

The wind blew and the weathercock turned. Then the weathercock was happy again. He was so happy that he sang most of the time. And always the song that he sang was this:

> "North or South,
>   Or East or West,
> I will always turn
>   As the wind thinks best!"

The Fox and the Grapes

ONE WARM day a fox was slinking through the woods. Now the fox was very thirsty, and when he saw some delicious grapes hanging in a cluster high on a vine, he felt he must have them.

He jumped and he jumped, but he could not jump high enough to reach the grapes. At last he grew tired of trying and went off, muttering to himself, "The grapes are probably sour, anyway."

Sometimes people are just as silly as that fox: When they cannot get what they want, they make believe there is something wrong with it.

Nail Broth

A WEARY tramp was plodding his way through a forest one day when he came upon a little cottage. Lights were shining through the windows and the tramp thought about the fire that was surely burning on the hearth and how good it would be to warm himself. He might even get something to eat, if he were lucky. So he went up to the door and knocked. An old woman opened the door.

"Good evening," said the tramp.

"Good evening," replied the woman. "Who are you, and what do you want?"

"I'm a traveler," the tramp told her. "I've been around the world and now I'm home again. I need a place to spend the night, and perhaps a bit of supper—"

"Well, you came to the wrong place for that," said the old woman. "This is not an inn, and as for food, why I haven't so much as a morsel in the whole house."

But the tramp begged so hard that at last the woman gave in and said he might lie on the floor for the night.

He thanked her and followed her into the warm house, where he saw at once that she was not as poor as she pretended to be. And as she went on and on, grumbling and complaining, he saw that she was a very stingy woman, the worst

he had ever met. He now made himself very agreeable, and asked her in his most charming manner if he might have something to eat.

"Where am I to get it from?" asked the woman. "I haven't tasted a morsel myself the whole day."

But the tramp was a cunning fellow, he was.

"You poor woman—you must be starving," he said. "Well, you shall have something with ME, then."

"Have something with YOU!" said the woman. "What has the likes of you to offer me?"

"Lend me a pot, and I'll show you," the tramp told her.

The old woman now became very curious, as you may guess, and so she let him have a pot. The tramp filled it with water and put it on the fire. Then he took a four-inch nail from his pocket and put it into the pot.

The woman stared and stared. "What are you making?" she asked.

"Nail broth," replied the tramp, and he began to stir the water with a spoon.

"Nail broth?" asked the woman.

"Yes, nail broth," said the tramp.

The old woman had seen and heard a great deal in her life, but that anyone could make broth with a nail—well, she had never heard the like before.

"What a thing for poor people to know," she said. "Will you show me how to make it?"

"Watch me and you'll learn how," said the tramp.

So the old woman watched with all her might while he went on stirring the broth.

"I'm afraid it may be a little thin this time," he said. "I have been making broth the whole week with the same nail. If I only had a handful of oatmeal, that would make it all right. But what one has to do without, it does no good to think about," he said, stirring the broth again.

"I think I can find a scrap of flour somewhere," said the woman, and she went to fetch some.

The tramp put the flour into the broth and went on stirring. "This broth would be good enough for company," he said, "if I only had a bit of salted beef and a few potatoes to put in. But what one has to do without, it does no good to think about."

Now the woman remembered that she did have a few potatoes and a piece of beef, too. These

The tramp went on stirring. Then suddenly he took out the nail. "It's ready," he said. "But with this kind of soup, the king and queen always have one sandwich at least. And they always have a cloth on the table when they eat. But what one has to do without, it does no good to think about."

But by now the woman had begun to feel quite grand. So she brought out butter and cheese, smoked beef and veal, and a cloth for the table, too, until at last the table looked as if it were decked out for company.

Never in her life had the old woman tasted such broth, and imagine, made only with a nail! She was in such good humor at having learned this easy way to make broth that she did not know how to make enough of the tramp for teaching her such a useful thing.

So they ate and ate until they became tired and sleepy. The tramp was now going to lie down on the floor. But that would never do, thought the old woman. "Such a grand person must sleep in a bed," she said.

The tramp did not need much pressing. He lay down on the bed and went to sleep. Next morning, when he woke, the first thing he got was coffee and a biscuit.

When he was leaving, the old woman gave him a bright dollar piece. "And many thanks for teaching me how to make broth with a nail," she said. "Now I can live in comfort."

"Well, it isn't very difficult if one only has something good to add to it," said the tramp as he went his way.

The woman stood at the door staring after him.

"Such people don't grow on every bush," she said. "If only there were more like him."

she gave to the tramp, who put them into the pot and went on stirring, while she sat and stared until her eyes almost burst their sockets.

"If one only had a little barley and a drop of milk," he said then, "one could ask the king himself to have some of this broth."

"Dear me! Ask the king to have some! Well, I never!" exclaimed the woman. And she remembered that she did have some barley, and a little milk, too. So she want to fetch both the one and the other.

Why Evergreens Keep Their Leaves

ONCE, very long ago, as winter was coming on, a poor little bird who had broken its wing and who could not fly with the other birds to the southland, where it was warm, hopped about among the trees of a great forest to ask for help.

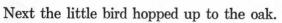

The first tree it came to was a birch. "Lovely birch tree," the bird said, "my wing is broken and I must find a place to keep warm. Will you permit me to live in your branches until spring?"

"No, no," answered the birch. "Why, I must take care of my leaves through the winter, and that alone will keep me quite busy. I can do nothing for you."

Next the little bird hopped up to the oak.

"Mighty oak tree," said the little bird in its nicest manner, "will you permit me to live in your branches until spring?"

"No, no," answered the oak. "Spring is a long time off and, for all I know, you might eat up my acorns. I think you had better leave."

Next the little bird hopped up to the willow tree.

"Gentle willow," the little bird said, "will you permit me to live in your branches until spring?"

"No, no," answered the willow. "I don't know you at all. Perhaps there are other trees somewhere that will take in strange birds—but not I. Please go away."

Now the little bird did not know where to turn, but it kept on hopping and fluttering along as best it could with its broken wing. Suddenly a voice asked, "Where are you going, little bird?"

The bird looked up and saw a friendly spruce tree, who had asked the question.

"I really don't know," said the bird sadly. "My wing is broken so that I cannot fly, and I must find a place to keep warm during the winter."

"Come live in one of my branches," invited the spruce tree. "You may stay all winter if you wish."

A pine tree stood beside the spruce.

"I am big and strong," he said. "I will help keep the wind off the little bird."

"I will give him berries to eat," said a juniper tree.

By and by the Frost King came. North Wind came with him.

North Wind found some leaves on the silver birch. He blew, till the leaves went fluttering down. He found some brown leaves on the oak. He blew, till he had spread them all on the ground beneath. He found some gold leaves on the willow. He blew them into the brook, and they sailed away like little gold ships.

"Now for the trees on the hill!" said North Wind.

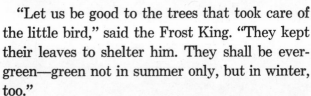

"Let us be good to the trees that took care of the little bird," said the Frost King. "They kept their leaves to shelter him. They shall be evergreen—green not in summer only, but in winter, too."

So the Frost King and North Wind were good to the spruce, the pine, and the juniper. They have kept their leaves green through every winter ever since.

113

The Turnip

ONE DAY a farmer planted a turnip, and from the seed there grew a big, beautiful turnip—the biggest, most beautiful turnip he had ever seen. And he began to try and pull up the turnip, and he pulled and pulled, but couldn't pull it up. So he called his wife to help him.

• •

And she caught hold of him, and he caught hold of the turnip, and they pulled and pulled, but couldn't pull it up.

Then his wife called their little granddaughter.

• •

And the farmer caught hold of the turnip, and his wife caught hold of him, and their grand-daughter caught hold of her, and they pulled and pulled, but couldn't pull it up.

Then the granddaughter called their dog, Sambo.

And the farmer caught hold of the turnip, his wife caught hold of him, their granddaughter caught hold of her, and Sambo caught hold of the granddaughter, and they pulled and pulled, but couldn't pull it up.

So then Sambo called the cat, Minnie.

And the farmer caught hold of the turnip, his wife caught hold of him, their granddaughter caught hold of her, Sambo caught hold of the granddaughter, and Minnie caught hold of Sambo, and they pulled and pulled, but couldn't pull it up.

Then Minnie the cat called Mr. Mouse.

And the farmer caught hold of the turnip, his wife caught hold of him, their granddaughter caught hold of her, Sambo caught hold of the granddaughter, Minnie caught hold of Sambo, and Mr. Mouse caught hold of Minnie, and they pulled and pulled and—pulled up the turnip!

The Golden Goose

THERE WAS once a man who had three sons. One day the eldest son packed a lunch and went into the forest to cut some wood. At midday he stopped work and sat down to eat. Just then a little old man appeared and said, "May I have a crust of bread and a glass of milk? I am famished and very thirsty." But the young man refused him. Now the little old man had magic powers, and he decided that anybody so selfish should be punished. And that is why, the next time the young man began chopping down a tree, he cut himself and had to go home to have his hand bandaged.

The next day the second son packed a lunch and went into the forest to cut some wood. And the little old man met him also and asked for something to eat and drink. Again he was refused, and so he punished the second son in the same way that he had the elder brother.

Then the youngest son, whose name was Dummling, decided that he too would go into the forest to cut some wood. But this time, when the little old man appeared and asked for something to eat and drink, he received a different answer. Dummling said, "I shall be only too glad to share my food with you." So they ate heartily, and when they had finished the little old man said: "Because you have been so kind, I shall reward you. Do you see that old tree over there? Cut it down and you will find something at the roots." Then he said goodby and went his way.

Dummling cut down the tree as he had been told, and lo and behold! at the roots he found a goose with feathers of pure gold. He carried the bird with him to an inn by the wayside where he was spending the night on his way home. Now the landlord of the inn had three daughters; and when they saw the beautiful goose, they felt they must have one of its golden feathers. So they waited until Dummling had fallen asleep, and then the eldest daughter seized the goose by one of its wings; but imagine her surprise when her hand stuck to the bird and she could not pull it away again! The second daughter tried to help her, but the instant she touched her sister she too was stuck fast. And the same thing happened to the third daughter. So there they were, all three of them, and they had to stay that way all night.

In the morning Dummling got up and went off with the goose under his arm, paying no attention to the three girls who were stuck fast to one another and to the goose. So wherever he traveled, they too were forced to follow.

They were crossing a field when a clergyman met them; and when he saw the procession he called out, "Girls shouldn't run after young men," and he took the youngest by the hand to lead her away. But as soon as he touched her, he stuck fast and had to follow. By and by, along came his assistant, saying, "Where are you going, sir? Have you forgotten there's a wedding today?" But the moment his hands touched the clergyman's gown, he too was stuck fast.

As the five were thus tripping along, one behind another, they met two ditch diggers coming home from work; and the clergyman cried out to them to help him. But scarcely had the ditch diggers laid hands on him than they too stuck to the others. And so there were seven all running together after Dummling and his goose.

Now Dummling thought he would see a little of the world before he went home; so he and his procession traveled on, till at last they came to a city where there was a king who had an only daughter. This princess had been ill for a long time, and nobody could make her laugh. The king had promised that any man who could make her smile should have her as his bride. When Dummling heard this, he went to her with his goose and all its procession. As soon as the princess saw the seven all stuck together, stumbling along and tripping on one another's heels, she burst out into peals of laughter. So Dummling married her and they lived happily ever after.

But what became of the goose and those who were stuck fast to it nobody ever did find out.

Jorinda and Joringel

THERE was once an old castle in the middle of a great forest, lived in by an old woman who was a witch. By day she made herself into a cat or an owl, but at night she became a woman again. When any man came within a hundred paces of the castle, he became motionless. He could not move from the place until she set him free. But when a young girl came within that distance, the witch changed her into a bird and put her into a cage, which she hung in a room in the castle. There were seven hundred cages of this kind, all with beautiful birds in them.

One day, a beautiful girl named Jorinda and a handsome youth named Joringel, who were planning to marry, went for a walk in the forest.

"Be careful," said Joringel. "We must not go too near the castle."

It was a lovely day. The late afternoon sun shone between the trees of the dark greenwood, and the turtledoves sang among the branches.

Jorinda and Joringel sat down side by side in the sunshine, to rest and talk of the future. Suddenly Joringel noticed that the sun was going down, and he turned to peer about into the bushes. He realized with a stab of fear that they were quite close to the old walls of the castle.

He turned to Jorinda, saying, "We had better start for home," and found her changed into a nightingale. An owl flew three times around them and screeched, "Whoo! Whoo! Whoo!" Joringel could not move. It was as if he had been turned to stone, and he could not speak or cry out. And now the sun had set. In the gloom the owl flew into a bush, and a moment later the old woman came out of it. She had big red eyes and a crooked nose whose tip reached her chin. She caught the nightingale and went away with it in her hand. Joringel could do nothing but watch them go, for he could not move.

At last the old woman came back and said in a droning voice:

> "The prisoner's fast,
> And her doom is cast,
>   So away! away!
> The charm is around her,
> The spell has bound her.
>   Go away! away!"

Joringel suddenly found that he was free. He fell on his knees before the witch and begged her to give Jorinda back to him. But she said he would never see her again. Joringel pleaded and wept, but all in vain. "Alas!" he cried. "What is to become of me now?"

At last he went away, stopping in a nearby village, where he found work as a shepherd. He often wandered in the forest around the castle, going as close to it as he dared. One night, he dreamed that he had found a red flower, in the middle of which was a large pearl. He plucked the flower and took it to the castle, and everything he touched with it was freed from the witch's spell.

In the morning, when he awoke, he began to search for the flower he had seen in his dream. He searched for eight days without success, but on the ninth day he found the flower. In the middle was a dewdrop as big as the pearl had been. He hurried to the castle with the flower and when he came within a hundred paces of the witch's home he found that he was not held fast as before, but walked right up to the door.

Overjoyed, Joringel touched the door with the flower and it flew open. He went in through the court, listening for the sound of birds. He went on and found the hall where the witch was feeding the birds in the seven hundred cages. When she saw Joringel she was very angry and rushed at him, hissing and shouting her magic words. But she could not come within two yards of him, for the flower protected him from her sorcery.

Joringel looked around at the birds. Alas, he thought, there were so many nightingales! How would he find Jorinda?

While he was thinking what to do, he noticed that the old woman was hurrying toward the door with one of the cages. He ran to her and touched her and the cage with the flower. At once the witch lost all her power, and Jorinda stood before him, beautiful as ever. She embraced Joringel and wept for joy.

Then Joringel changed all the other birds back into maidens again, and went home with Jorinda. They were married soon after, and lived happily together for many, many years.

The Old Woman
and Her Pig

AN OLD WOMAN was sweeping her house and she found a little crooked sixpence. "What," said she, "shall I do with this sixpence? I will go to the market and buy a pig." As she was going home, she came to a stile; but the piggy would not go over the stile.

She went a little farther, and she met a dog. So she said to the dog, "Dog, bite pig; piggy won't go over the stile, and I shan't get home tonight." But the dog would not.

She went a little farther, and she met a stick. So she said, "Stick, stick, beat dog; dog won't bite pig, piggy won't go over the stile, and I shan't get home tonight." But the stick would not.

She went a little farther, and she met a fire. So she said, "Fire, fire, burn stick; stick won't beat dog, dog won't bite pig, pig won't go over the stile, and I shan't get home tonight." But the fire would not.

She went a little farther, and she met some water. So she said, "Water, water, quench fire; fire won't burn stick, stick won't beat dog, dog won't bite pig, pig won't go over the stile, and I shan't get home tonight."

But the water would not.

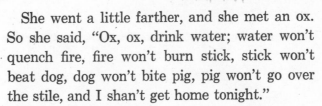

She went a little farther, and she met an ox. So she said, "Ox, ox, drink water; water won't quench fire, fire won't burn stick, stick won't beat dog, dog won't bite pig, pig won't go over the stile, and I shan't get home tonight."

But the ox would not.

She went a little farther, and she met a butcher. So she said, "Butcher, butcher, kill ox; ox won't drink water, water won't quench fire, fire won't burn stick, stick won't beat dog, dog won't bite pig, pig won't go over the stile, and I shan't get home tonight."

But the butcher would not.

She went a little farther, and she met a rope. So she said, "Rope, rope, hang butcher; butcher won't kill ox, ox won't drink water, water won't quench fire, fire won't burn stick, stick won't beat dog, dog won't bite pig, pig won't go over the stile, and I shan't get home tonight."

But the rope would not.

She went a little farther, and she met a rat. So she said, "Rat, rat, gnaw rope; rope won't hang butcher, butcher won't kill ox, ox won't drink water, water won't quench fire, fire won't burn stick, stick won't beat dog, dog won't bite pig, pig won't go over the stile, and I shan't get home tonight."

But the rat would not.

She went a little farther, and she met a cat. So she said, "Cat, cat, catch rat; rat won't gnaw rope, rope won't hang butcher, butcher won't kill ox, ox won't drink water, water won't quench fire, fire won't burn stick, stick won't beat dog, dog won't bite pig, pig won't go over the stile, and I shan't get home tonight."

123

But the cat said to her, "If you will go to yonder cow and fetch me a saucer of milk, I will catch the rat." So away went the old woman to the cow.

But the cow said to her, "If you will go to yonder haystack, and bring me a handful of hay, I will give you the milk." So away went the old woman to the haystack, and she brought the hay to the cow.

As soon as the cat had lapped up the milk, the cat began to catch the rat, the rat began to gnaw the rope, the rope began to hang the butcher, the butcher began to kill the ox, the ox began to drink the water, the water began to quench the fire, the fire began to burn the stick, the stick began to beat the dog, the dog began to bite the pig, and the little pig jumped over the stile.

And so the woman got home that night.

The End